MYSTIC PIECES

SHADY GROVE MYSTERIES, BOOK 1

ADA BELL

WELCOME TO SHADY GROVE...

Aly doesn't believe in psychics. Too bad she just had a vision.

Future scientists don't have visions. Aly's got enough on her plate, with finishing her degree and taking care of her nephew and starting her new job at the antique store while drooling over the owner's gorgeous son. No visions.

Alas, the universe doesn't care what Aly believes. When she turns 21, she starts to feel psychic impressions left on objects. A disorienting power for someone surrounded by antiques. Then cranky customer Earl is killed, and Aly's new boss Olive is the prime suspect. Who hated Earl enough to kill? Police would rather make a quick arrest than investigate, so it's up to Aly to clear Olive's name.

Shady Grove is reeling from the first murder in decades. If Aly can get her hands on the murder weapon, she should be able to solve the crime. Can she learn to control her visions before the killer sets their sights on her?

To Kellye,

Who is one of the kindest, most giving people I know,
an amazing auntie, and a terrific writer.
Thank you for helping me turn my coal into diamonds.

and

To Tracie,

Because this series wouldn't exist
if you didn't believe in me.

1

Most people went drinking to celebrate their twenty-first birthday. Me? Job hunting in eleven-degree temperatures. This never would've happened if I'd stayed in California. Over the past few weeks, I'd learned the hard way that the types of jobs I was qualified for didn't get posted online. Welcome to Shady Grove, New York. We didn't even have a Starbucks. I'd need to walk around and physically talk to people about hiring me, like someone living in the 1950s.

No one ever said I didn't know how to have a good time.

Actually, now that I thought about it, people said that a lot. I spent most of my time home alone with my brother and his three-year-old son. But not drinking wasn't my fault. Shady Grove didn't have a bar, and until I got a job, there was no way to get to the next town over.

Main Street had been built a couple hundred years ago and never updated. Cobblestones still lined the streets, and the sidewalks were made of raised wood. Wooden awnings protected shoppers from the elements, with matching signs hanging down to advertise each business. A cozy area to work, no doubt.

The first six places I went to request an application nearly defeated me. Three weren't hiring; two were permanently closed due to the recession. The magic shop didn't post hours, and I'd never seen a person there. Last year, someone started a rumor that I Put a Spell on You ran a front for a money-laundering operation. After all, did anyone still believe in magic?

When the cold started to get to me, I took a break and headed over to On What Grounds?. Since it sat adjacent to Main Street, the one and only caffeine hole in town bore the same quaint look, right down to the wooden frame and red and white striped awnings over the giant plate-glass windows. In the summer, they would set up bistro tables outside, but no one was masochistic enough to use them in January.

I managed to hit the store between the pre-work rush and the mid-morning rush, so it was relatively quiet. The only one working was the manager, Rusty. We'd gone on two extremely unexciting dates not long after I moved to town. Barely spoken outside the coffee shop since. He was cute, which is why I'd gone out with him. His wire-rimmed glasses and spiky black hair gave him a Daniel Radcliffe vibe. Even better when he had a couple of days' worth of stubble, like now. Brown eyes, long lashes, and a devastatingly adorable dimple in his left cheek. Not into me at all.

"Hey, Aly. Where's Kyle?" For the past year, my three-year-old nephew came with me everywhere I went. After all, I'd moved here to help Kevin after my sister-in-law died. "Everything okay?"

"Great!" I said. "He started preschool, so I'm free in the

mornings. Actually, I'm looking for a job. You're not by any chance hiring, are you?"

There wasn't a sign in the window, but I had to ask. This morning couldn't be a total loss.

He shook his head. "Sorry, no. Does this mean you're not heading back to California? I always figured you wouldn't be around for long."

It was on the tip of my tongue to ask if that was why things didn't work out between us, but now wasn't the time to rehash our failed relationship. Instead, I said, "No, I enrolled at Maloney College. They've got a great program, and it's time to finish my degree."

"Cool." He grinned at me. "Try Olive's place, around the corner. I hear she's looking for someone."

I thanked him for the tip and downed my small coffee as fast as possible without burning my tongue. A few minutes later, I braced myself for the cold and headed out, stuffing my hands in my pockets and wishing I could find my gloves. As promised, when I rounded the corner onto Main Street, a sign hung in the window of a store I'd never paid much attention to. To be fair, though, I pretty much didn't go anywhere other than to playdates and baby gymnastics. Which wasn't hiring—I'd asked.

The battered shingle advertised a shop named "Missing Pieces," whatever that meant. Not that it mattered; they needed a worker. I'd go in even if they sold only objects with holes in them.

The sign itself did not instill confidence in me. "HELP WANTED: Must be open-minded."

Open-minded about what? Like, the owner dyed her hair a different color every week, or she sometimes sacrificed goats after they shut down for the day?

But jobs didn't grow on trees in Shady Grove, and I'd been without one too long. When I first moved here, Kevin had paid my bills, but now that Kyle started preschool, it was time to support myself. My brother was very generous, but I hated relying on him. I needed an independent income. Something where, when I spent an afternoon with my nephew, it was because I wanted to, and not because I needed the cash. Also, college classes started in two weeks, and if I couldn't pay for a car, I couldn't get to campus.

Back to Missing Pieces. I stared at the help wanted sign for another twenty seconds or so, but my mind was already made up. Unless "being open-minded" meant making porn in the shop's basement, it was this or delivering newspapers. The latter option inspired zero enthusiasm in me, both because it required getting up at four o'clock in the morning and because it paid per subscriber. In a town of roughly ten thousand people where most everyone got their news online, a paper route would barely buy the umbrella I'd need to keep my hair dry while walking around town. It rained a lot in Shady Grove.

Element number one was hydrogen. H. Number two was helium. He.

When I got nervous, I recited the elements of the periodic table in my head. It soothed me.

With a deep sigh, I smoothed my hair back with one hand and pushed the door open with the other. I didn't know what a store called "Missing Pieces" would offer, but there was only one way to find out. Personally, I hoped for puzzles. As long as they weren't literally missing pieces.

Jingling bells above the door welcomed me. The store was darker inside than I'd expected, especially with the giant windows, probably because it was utterly crammed full. Sunlight had no way to penetrate the room. I'd never seen so much cool stuff all in one space. Furniture filled every available spot on the floor, except for the clothing rack by the far wall. Bookshelves overflowed with old volumes that my fingers itched to explore. To my left, an entire display case full of old tea sets would have made my mom swoon with joy. On the right sat a disorganized mess: a birdcage; one of those screens that divided a room; a child's red, wooden Radio Flyer wagon. Hmm. Kyle might like that. I wondered how much it cost. But one thing at a time.

"Hello dear. Can I help you?" I turned to find a woman who appeared to be about fifty, with long dark hair parted in the center and pulled back into a bun at the nape of her neck. Dark liner rimming her blue eyes made them look enormous. She wore a high-necked lemon-colored dress. The old-fashioned kind with a hoop skirt and matching parasol. Maybe being open-minded meant not commenting on her outfits? I could live with that.

"Oh, I'm sorry. I'm just—"

"Don't let the dress fool you, sweetie." She laughed, a warm sound that made me like her instantly. "I'm trying to find something for a charity costume ball. I don't normally walk around looking like I stepped out of the Civil War. My name is Olive. I own this place."

Well, that was a relief.

"It's nice to meet you. I'm Aly Reynolds." I gestured toward the window. "I'm here about the job."

"Oh, yes, of course!" She took a deep breath and waved at her face with one of those old fans I'd only ever seen in the movies. "Goodness, this is the warmest garment I've ever worn. No wonder everyone needed smelling salts back then. They must've been constantly dropping from heat exhaustion. Why don't you fill out an application and take a look around while I change?"

Hopefully she wouldn't take long, because I saw myself getting lost in here, looking at all the amazing treasures. If I ventured in much further, I'd need a trail of bread crumbs to find my way back.

Beside the counter holding the register sat a patio bistro set. It seemed both out-of-place inside the store and yet fitting. Nice table, with a white marble top and fancy curved metal legs. It was something you might find on the sidewalk at a little cafe in Paris. The chairs had matching backs and legs, with gold cushions the same color as the veins in the marble. It didn't look terribly comfortable, but it was beautiful.

Since it was the only place to sit, I pulled out a chair and got to work. The paper Olive had handed me was only a page, and with my paltry work history, it didn't take long to get to the end. There was no sign of her, so I left the finished application on the table and went to explore the shop.

I wandered through the rows, marveling at an old settee here, an armoire there. Unfortunately, the guest room at my brother's house didn't have a lot of room for extra furniture. My sister-in-law Katrina had furnished her and Kevin's McMansion near New York City when they bought it. Some fancy suburb I could never remember the name of, probably since Kevin worked so many hours as a lawyer, I'd never managed to visit. Since I'd been living in a student's apartment at the time, I arrived in Shady Grove with not much more than my laptop, my clothes, and my books. What else did a person need? We had a lot of empty rooms, but filling them up hadn't been high on our priority list.

The price tags told me it was a good thing I didn't have a strong desire to own antique furniture. But it was cool to think about working here, helping this stuff find homes. Sit on the plush velvet settee and fan myself sometimes, like the heroine in a historical romance. Possibly wearing a dress like the one Olive was currently changing out of. Without the corset.

At the thought, I glanced toward the doorway she had disappeared through, but I didn't hear anything. That dress had about six thousand buttons down the back; I should have offered to help. Maybe this was her interview test, where she was waiting to see if I was nice enough to offer or to check on her when she didn't return.

Turning the corner, I found myself face to face with the most fabulously gorgeous jewelry display I'd ever seen in my life. Rings, earrings, bracelets, cuff links? A dazzling array of colors, metals, and gems. This was way more my speed—most of what you'd find in a shop like this should be costume stuff. Completely affordable.

A particular piece caught my eye, shining and shimmering at me from its maroon velvet box. The ring practically glowed in the dim light, sending out a beacon as strong as if it called my name. I couldn't tear my eyes away.

It wasn't the fanciest piece in the glass case or the largest, but the glimmering opal drew me in. My finger itched to see how the item would feel.

Hanging out with a three-year-old all day made most jewelry impractical. Kyle wasn't into dress-up. The ring probably didn't fit. If it wasn't fake, I couldn't afford it. A million excuses went through my mind, but none of them mattered. Before I could talk myself out of it, I picked up the ring and slid the gold band over the fourth finger of my right hand. It fit so perfectly, it might have been made for me.

Lightning hit me. My entire body jolted. Energy zapped

through me, leaving tingles from head to toe. Instantly, my mind was transported. The store fell away. No more jewelry case, no more rose-patchouli scent or gently piped-in classical music. I didn't know where I was, but I couldn't move.

In front of me, my hands wrapped around a worn leather steering wheel. On the other side of the windshield, headlights barely penetrated the darkness. My entire body jerked from side-to-side as the steering wheel fought my grip. Everything spun.

Trees streamed by the window, until one popped up directly in front of me.

We were going to crash!

Beside me, someone gasped. Something hit the back of my neck, hard. My vision blurred. My ears roared, and that terrible scream kept echoing. Blood gurgled in my throat. I choked.

What was happening?

Pain lanced my entire body. A scream rang out.

But the horrible noise wasn't in the store. It came from inside me. Only low, tortured sounds escaped my mouth. I jumped, shaking my head as if doing so could make all the horrible sensations go away. My fingers tore at the ring. I didn't know why or how, but I needed to get it off me.

"Aly?" Olive's voice penetrated the fog, sounding a million miles away. I lunged toward the sound.

The world returned to normal. The glass case in front of me came into focus, the rows of merchandise created walls, and only the sound of my breathing filled the space. I touched one hand to the back of my skull, but everything felt normal. Nothing to explain the pain, the blood. My fingers came away clean, like the wound only existed in my imagination.

Open-minded? Nope. No, thanks. Not me. I didn't need a job this badly. *I'm out.* Shady Grove Globe, *here I come.*

"Aly! There you are." Olive turned the corner from the main aisle into my row, now dressed in jeans and a green t-shirt. She looked like a completely different person. If she'd heard my scream, she must be a remarkably talented actress. "I see you found your ring."

2

The grandfather clock ticked off the seconds as Olive and I stared at each other. The longer the silence stretched between us, the more concerned her face became. But still, her words didn't make any sense. I couldn't speak until she repeated herself.

"You've got your ring?"

"There's been a mistake," I said. "I found this ring in the case and tried it on. It isn't mine."

"Of course it is." She stared at my shaking hands for a long moment before her eyes traveled up to my face. "What's wrong? Most people are excited to find items that suit them."

"An item 'that suits me'? Are you joking?" I spit the words at her while yanking that stupid thing off my finger. Well, I tried. It stuck. "What was that? What happened to me?"

"Unless I'm mistaken, you're the one I've been waiting for. And I'm rarely mistaken."

I shook my head. "No. I'm just looking for a job. I don't know what you're talking about. Sorry. I should go."

Then I did the only thing that made sense. I yanked at the band a second time, but nothing happened. I couldn't breathe. I couldn't think. The more I tried to get the ring off, the harder it clutched my finger.

Olive took a step toward me, and I panicked.

Ducking past her, I ran.

"Aly, stop!" Her voice rang out behind me, but I ignored her. Throwing the front door open, I tore through it.

About two feet down the sidewalk, I bounced off a brick wall. No, wait. A guy. A very good-looking guy, now that I stopped to look at him. Tall, but not too tall. A hint of stubble along his jaw, with spiky light brown hair and a crooked smile that somehow eased my blind panic. Under any other circumstances, I'd have stopped to talk to him.

"Whoa, there!" he said. "Where's the fire?"

"I'm sorry—I can't—I have to..." Words bubbled out of me, not making a lick of sense. My face burned.

"Are you okay?"

I opened my mouth, but nothing happened. Here I was talking to the best-looking guy I'd seen since moving to Shady Grove, and my brain couldn't even form a sentence. It didn't matter. Behind me, the welcome bells at Missing Pieces jingled, signaling the arrival of Olive. Before I could finish my barely-formed apology, my feet took me down the street a second time.

About three blocks away, my senses returned, and I slowed to a halt. First of all, I didn't know what the ring cost, but by racing out of the store wearing it, I'd just shoplifted for the first time in my life. After giving the store owner my name, address, telephone number, social security number, and references. Great move, Aly.

It didn't matter that the ring attacked my senses. My reaction wasn't rational. Shame burned through me. As a would-be scientist, rational was my middle name. Heck, with parents who gave me a name like Aluminum, I was lucky it wasn't my first name. At least "Aluminum" shortened to something cute. Poor Kelvin had to go to court and get a legal name change the day he turned eighteen. Mom still hadn't forgiven him, but I was firmly Team Kevin on this one. There are lots of ways to instill a love of science in your kids without giving them weird names. No wonder my brother went into law instead.

Number three was lithium. Li. Also Kevin's favorite old album. Number four was beryllium. Be. Number five was.... I couldn't remember element number five. Now was not the time. I needed to calm down.

Forcing myself to inhale slowly, I turned around in the direction I'd come. The sidewalk was empty. No one followed me. Neither Olive nor the guy I'd plowed through were anywhere to be seen.

What happened back there? Something drew me to the ring, I put it on, and—I experienced some kind of psychotic break? A hallucination? If it was either of those things, then the timing must be a coincidence. To the best of my (very limited) knowledge, medical events weren't generally associated with people trying on jewelry. I mean, I was no doctor, but that never once happened on *Grey's Anatomy*. There must be a reasonable explanation.

It must've been my imagination that kept the ring stuck to my finger back in the store. With a sigh, I leaned against the low wall separating the wooden sidewalk from Main Street. This time, when my fingers closed around the cool metal, it slid easily over my knuckle and came off in my hand.

I held it up to the light, examining it. A large oval-shaped opal, sparkling where the sun hit it, set into a gold band. Gorgeous. Hopefully also inexpensive, since I'd accidentally stolen it.

In other news, it seemed unlikely that Olive would offer me a job now. Darn it. Maybe Kevin would let me take his car over to Willow Falls this weekend.

One thing at a time. I needed to go back to Missing Pieces and return the ring. I certainly didn't want to keep it, and if I dropped it down the storm drain, I'd have to pay for it. With my luck, it probably cost five hundred dollars.

A voice in my head suggested putting the ring back on to see if the same thing happened a second time, but—no. No way, no how. I'd rather put on a Boston Red Sox jersey and run through the Bronx.

As much as I wanted to drop the thing and keep running, my inner moral compass insisted I go back and apologize. The ring needed to be returned, and I couldn't just stick it in the mail. Also my inner paranoia, because the last thing I needed was for the post office to lose the envelope, causing Olive to send the police knocking on my door.

Boron! That was element five. Symbol B. See? I was fine.

With a deep, fortifying breath, I turned and marched back to Missing Pieces. The hot guy I'd barreled through on my way out of the building was nowhere in sight. Thankfully, neither was Olive. Holding my head high, I pushed the door open and walked back into the store as if I belonged there.

The bells over the door jingled. I was starting to enjoy that chime. It was peaceful. Calming. Something I desperately needed. For a second, I considered staying there, opening and shutting the door another thirty times or so until I felt really Zen. Element six was carbon. C.

No such luck. Olive spotted me immediately.

"Aly! I'm so glad you came back. You worried me."

My face turned so red, I actually saw the tip of my nose lighting up. It took all the dignity I could muster to hold one arm out stiffly. "I seem to have forgotten to take this off when I left. My apologies."

"Oh, please." She waved one hand. "It's fine. We should talk more."

I shook my head. "That's not a good idea. I need to see a doctor."

"Not feeling well?"

You could say that. Well, she did say that. I would've said that I was suffering a psychotic break, but this stranger wasn't the person to confide in. Unless she knew where I could find a good therapist in Shady Grove. Possibly the only therapist. Oh, man. I needed to get out of here.

Element seven was nitrogen. N.

As if she could sense that I was about to bolt again, Olive approached slowly and put one hand on my arm. "Please stay. My son is making tea. We need to have a chat."

How would her son feel about me coming in and taking his tea? "It's okay. I don't want the job anymore."

She tilted her head at me. "Is that true? Or are you scared because something happened when you put on my grandmother's ring?"

I narrowed my eyes at her. How could she—?

Oh. Suddenly it all made sense. A trick ring. People put it on; they had visions. I wondered how she did it—a liquid applied to the inside of the metal? Or maybe the whole thing was a show. Maybe the lights did flicker, someone did scream, and something really did bonk the back of my head. Perhaps when Olive wrote "open-minded" on the sign, she meant, "Must be willing to star in unscripted horror movies."

This could even be a Shady Grove rite of passage, where all the old-timers knew about it. Not having a psychotic break, then. No brain damage. I didn't need an MRI.

I forced a laugh. "Yup. Cool trick. Is that the only joke item you sell?"

"Joke item?"

The hot guy from the street appeared from the back, carrying a wooden tray. The fragile teapot, tiny china cups, and cookies looked out-of-place in his strong hands.

I started at the sight of him. "What are you doing here?"

"Me? Just serving tea. What are you doing here?"

Belatedly, I realized that I still had no idea who he was or why he was here, bringing me tea. "Sorry. I forgot my manners. I'm Aly."

"Sam is my son," Olive said. "Sam, Aly applied for the cashier's job. We were just about to have a little chat and get to know one another."

"Cool. I'll leave you to it. I've got some work to do, and the record starts at four."

"You're making a record? Do you sing?"

From the burst of laughter escaping both Olive and Sam, I deduced that he wasn't a musician. My cheeks flamed.

When Sam caught the look on my face, the amusement faded. "I'm sorry. No, no, I'm not. I couldn't carry a tune with a forklift. There's a guy going for the World Record of most digits of pi memorized. It's a big deal down in the City, at least in my circles, and I want to watch."

"That sounds so cool! Have fun."

"Thanks." He set the tray on the bistro table where I'd filled out my application, then disappeared into the back before I could pepper him with questions, like why had I never seen him around town and what was his favorite color and how many children would he like to have with me?

Finally, I realized that I was staring. I forced my attention away from the empty doorway. "Does Sam work here with you?" *Please, please, please say yes.*

Olive laughed. "Oh, no. He's getting his MBA down in New York City. He's just visiting for a few days. Came up to help me and my wife move some things."

A shame. A job that came with a side of eye candy would be nice. Not that I had time for dating. Between Kevin and Kyle, my life was plenty full. We had playdates and movie nights and blanket forts and all the things a girl could desire. Except, you know, smooching. But I could always watch *The Princess Bride.*

"Please, take off your coat and have a seat."

I debated leaving my coat on in case I needed to make another quick getaway, but winter gear in New York was no joke. After about two minutes in the store, I was already sweating. If I started drinking tea while wearing my L.L. Bean puffy coat, I'd be having heat-generated hallucinations in no time at all. One disturbing, out-of-nowhere vision a day was enough for me.

We moved to the table, which unfortunately only had two chairs. Sam wouldn't be joining us. Olive picked up the teapot and filled both cups. I waved away her offers of milk and sugar. "So, Aly, tell me about yourself. Do you consider yourself to be open-minded?"

Wait. Was she resetting our interview? She acted like I'd just walked in and asked for the job, without the intervening incident. I wasn't sure I wanted to work here anymore. I was about to say so when a little voice pointed out that if I talked to her, Olive might give me some clues about my out-of-body experience or whatever happened.

"The easy answer is yes, but no one really considers themselves close-minded." She smiled, so I continued, "I have an associate's degree in biology, so I'm all about experimentation and changing my mind to fit the facts. Is that what you mean?"

"Not exactly, but it is nice to know you're willing to admit when you're wrong." She paused. "Strange things sometimes happen in Shady Grove, particularly in this store. I need someone who can go with the flow, not get too flustered."

An image of me racing out of the store flashed before my eyes, and my cheeks grew warm. But Olive let me back in the store, offered me tea, and was giving me another chance to interview. She must have her reasons. "When you say strange things, do you mean, like—visions?"

"Maybe. The important thing is that you're willing to consider possibilities outside your realm of experience."

"That's why I came back," I said. "And why I'm still hoping you'll give me a job."

I needed to know what happened to me, and while I could just come out and ask, I preferred to get to know Olive first. See if she was trust-worthy. She was unusual, but she didn't seem dangerous. Then again, neither did Ted Bundy.

She glanced at my application, which I'd forgotten about leaving on the table earlier. "You're originally from California?"

I nodded. "Sacramento. I grew up there."

"That's a long way from Shady Grove."

"Yeah. My older brother took over the town's only law practice not long ago. He used to be a big, fancy lawyer in New York City."

"You're Kevin's sister?"

I don't know why it surprised me she'd know that. It was a small town, after all. "Yeah. He's nine years older, and he left for college when I was a kid, so in some ways, we're just getting to know each other."

"He moved here after his wife died, right?" When I nodded, she clucked her tongue. "Such a tragedy."

A little over a year ago, my brother returned home from work to find his house locked and his wife Katrina lying at the bottom of the stairs, dead. The only other person around was then-two-year-old Kyle. Police found signs of a struggle, but no suspects. None of which I wanted to get into, so I simply murmured a sound of agreement.

"And you're not planning to return to California?"

"Oh, no," I assured her. "I'm taking classes at Maloney College when the spring semester starts next month. It's not a big school, but they have a great science program. It's time to finish my education. I'll be in Shady Grove for at least another two years while I get my bachelor's degree in biology."

She returned to my application. "It says here you used to work in the college bookstore, so you must know your way around retail."

"Yes!" I told her about my love of books and helping people and deftly avoided mentioning the fact that, since Shady Grove didn't have a mall, my options for working retail were basically here or the pet store.

They'd turned me down.

"Everything looks great." She peered at me over the top of her bifocals before glancing back down at my resume. "I do have to contact your references, of course, but if it all checks out, I think it's safe to say you could start tomorrow after lunch."

An enormous wave of relief washed over me. "Wonderful! Thank you so much."

"You're welcome," she said. "I just have one more question for you."

"Anything. I'm an open book."

"When did you first learn that you're psychic?"

3

My cup clattered onto the saucer, sending tea sloshing over the side. I stared at Olive without blinking for several long seconds. She waited patiently, hands clasped in her lap as if she'd just asked me to pass her a lump of sugar.

"When did I who the what now?" I finally squeaked out.

She chuckled. "There's no need to play coy with me. Nothing else could have put that look on your face earlier."

That stupid ring. I sputtered for what felt like hours until she put me out of my misery.

"I'm sorry. Maybe you didn't know. You have a gift."

I shook my head. "That's impossible. There's no such thing as that kind of gift. Psychics or mystics or seers or whatever aren't real."

"Are you sure about that?" She patted her hair, her cheeks, her chest. "I certainly think I'm real. If I'm imaginary, I'd like you to imagine I play the piano beautifully. I always wanted to learn, but I'm all thumbs."

This day just kept getting weirder. Maybe I'd fallen

asleep on the walk to the store, and I passed out in a ditch somewhere.

"You're telling me you're psychic? Like those women on TV who tell you all about your long-lost love?"

She shook her head. "I'm not a tele-psychic. I have certain extrasensory gifts, and unless I miss my mark, so do you."

Time to go. I was a biology student. Future scientists didn't have extrasensory gifts. We were the people who proved that those things didn't exist! Yet, instead of pushing my chair back and heading home, somehow, I heard myself say, "That ring... I thought it was a trick. A hallucinogen on the inside of the band, maybe. People put it on, they see things."

"Some people, sure," Olive said. "Not most. That experience is reserved for people like us. We're a tiny percentage of the overall population."

"So what you're saying is, when you put on that ring, you saw a woman's death? Heard the screams, felt the pain in the back of your head, tasted blood? Because if so, let me tell you, lady, you should not have put it out on the floor for poor, unsuspecting customers to find."

Her eyes widened. "Goodness no! Is that what happened?"

Now I was just too confused to speak, so I nodded.

"How horrible for you." Olive tsked softly under her breath as she refilled our teacups. I resisted the urge to ask her to put something stronger in mine. "They say everyone's gift is unique. When I touch certain items, use my gift, I get a vision of the true owner. A flash, usually. Not much. I've had that ring for years. As I said earlier, it belonged to my grandmother. But this morning, I couldn't stop thinking about it. Something told me that ring needed to go out on the shelves immediately.

When I put it on, I saw a flash of curly chestnut hair, a smat-tering of freckles, and I caught a whiff of hazelnuts."

Whoa, there. Hold on. "Seriously? Hazelnuts."

"Yeah, why. Do you have an allergy?"

"More like an addiction. I eat Nutella toast for breakfast every morning."

"Well, there you go. The same sense told me it was time to hire an assistant. The moment I saw you, I knew." She picked the ring up from where it sat beside her plate and held it out to me. "Here, I'd like you to have this. No charge."

"Uh-uh. No way. I don't want anything to do with it."

"Out of all the objects in the entire store, why did you go to this ring, specifically? Why did you try it on?"

That was easy. "I tried it on because it's beautiful."

"There are many beautiful rings back there. The opal called to you."

The things she was saying made no sense. Magic rings that called to people and gave them visions were stuff from fairy tales. I believed in the real world, a world of science and vaccines and...rings that made me see things? No way. Maybe I had an iron deficiency.

Or maybe, a little voice in the back of my mind insisted, I should listen to Olive and hear what she had to say. I believed in facts and logic. But at the moment, logic didn't apply to the facts. The person who understood what happened might be sitting right in front of me. If I wasn't going to run straight to the local hospital and demand an MRI, I should take the time to think about what she was telling me.

"When did you know I was going to pick that ring?" I asked.

"Not until you walked through the door. And I didn't

know what would happen. I just had a strong sense that I should shine up the gold opal, put it out in the front of the display case, then hang a Help Wanted sign. And here you are."

Here I was. Confused, freaked out, and undoubtedly in the store, just as she knew I would be. Which made no sense. There had to be some rational explanation for all of this. Like, Olive was running an elaborate scam to get me to trust her so she could steal... the eleven dollars in my bank account? It seemed like such a nefarious plot would be better researched.

"Hold on," I said. "So you're not really hiring?"

"I am now," she said. "Only very certain people have the skills I'm looking for in an employee."

"And I have those skills?" My first instinct was to be flattered, but if she only hired psychics, then her interest in me was as random as a lightning strike.

"Tell me again what happened when you put on the ring. You saw a woman get hurt?"

I shook my head. I didn't want to talk about it. All I wanted was a long bubble bath and the latest episode of *General Hospital* on my tablet.

"If you tell me, I might be able to help."

My gut told me to trust Olive. Although I wanted to believe in a rational explanation for what happened when I put on the ring, everything she'd said made sense.

"How do I know you won't think I'm crazy? What I felt... it can't be real."

Instead of arguing with me, she leaned back and took a sip of her tea. After deliberately placing the cup back on the saucer, she said, "Why not?"

"Because I haven't had anything to drink today, I don't do

drugs, and I'm not taking any prescription medications. I don't believe in visions."

"Not believing in something doesn't make it untrue. How many people do you know who don't believe in science?"

Touché. Funny, of all the things she could have said, that was probably the number one way to make me stay. She could have laughed things off. She could have talked about powers and mysticism. But instead, she gave me an argument I couldn't refute.

I took a deep breath. "I don't know how to explain it. Nothing like this has ever happened to me before. I put on the ring. Suddenly, I went somewhere else. Not physically. My feet were still on the floor here. But the walls were gone. The lights were gone. Instead of the rose oil and patchouli of the shop, I smelled something different. I don't know what it was. Or where."

"The ring wanted to show you something."

"But how? Why me? And why now?"

Olive clucked her tongue sympathetically. "I'm afraid I don't know, exactly. The gift is different for everyone. But I believe when you put on my grandmother's ring, you had a vision of her."

The hair on my arms stood up. "This is ridiculous. I touch other people's things all the time. Nothing ever happened. I'm sitting on your chair now. It's not me. I'm not magic. There's no such thing as magic."

"On that, we'll have to agree to disagree. As to why this happened now, it's hard to say. Some people show powers from a very young age. Personally, my gifts didn't manifest until my twenty-first birthday."

My eyes widened. She couldn't know. My date of birth wasn't on the application. We had never met, and I hadn't given her my ID yet. I knew about four people in this town, and I doubted my brother was walking around telling anyone the day I was born.

The sincerity in her voice told me Olive believed the things she was saying. Maybe we both needed MRIs. Maybe the hospital in Willow Falls would give us a two-for-one discount.

There was one more thing I needed to know, and I didn't know a good way to ask. "How did your grandmother die?"

"Car accident. She fell asleep at the wheel on her way home from Bingo and drove into oncoming traffic."

The flash of lightning—oncoming headlights? The pain on the back of my head. The screams. The blood choking me. It all fit. And yet, there was no way I could have known.

"The other car—there was a woman in the other car?"

She nodded, her voice suddenly grave. "Did you see the accident?"

"Not just see. I *felt* it."

"Oh my! That's terrible." Her eyes filled with tears, reminding me that we weren't just talking about some random old lady. It was her grandmother.

"I'm so sorry, Olive." Suddenly, I felt nauseated. "Is there a restroom I can use?"

"Yes, of course. Take your time." She pointed to the doorway where Sam had disappeared earlier. "First door on the left."

Olive's directions led me to a tiny but functional restroom with barely enough space to turn around. Books crammed into every available space and a bathrobe on the back of the door told me this room wasn't intended for customer use. After locking the door, I sat on the closed toilet lid for several minutes, taking deep breaths and praying that my lunch wouldn't make a reappearance. Splashing cold water on my face helped a little.

I could do this. Something happened that was way beyond my comfort zone. To figure out what it was, I had a hypothesis: I might have some kind of powers I'd previously been unaware of. Or believed in. The next step was to test that hypothesis. To do that, I needed to leave the bathroom, go home, and think about all of this logically.

Making a plan helped. I liked plans. After rinsing my mouth out, I went back to thank Olive for the opportunity and say goodbye. Our interview was done. Time to go do some research.

She'd retaken her place behind the register, so she must've realized that our conversation was over. "Are you okay?"

"Honestly, I don't know. But I think I will be. Do you still want to hire me?"

She waved one hand. "Don't be silly. Of course I do. You've discovered something new about yourself, and it's scary. I get that. But I can help you. The question is, do you still want to work here?"

Part of me wanted to say no. To leave and pretend none of this ever happened. However, no one else I'd talked to was hiring, and Maloney College was about an hour's drive away. Gas cost money. As did a car, which I currently didn't have. I couldn't afford to walk away, for more reasons than one.

Footsteps sounded beyond the rear door, and Sam appeared in the doorway. Without his hat, scarf, and puffy coat, he looked even more handsome than he had outside. Too bad he barely spared me a glance.

"Hey," he said. "I'm just about done, so I'm heading out."

"Do you want lunch first?"

"No thanks, I'm still full from that six-course breakfast Mama made. I'll see you soon." He kissed her on the cheek, and I swooned. A grown man who wasn't shy about showing affection to his mother in front of strangers? Be still my heart. "Nice to meet you, Aly."

"You, too," I barely squeaked out as he moved toward the coat rack to prepare to head outside.

"Bye, sweetie. Thanks for helping with the bookcases."

"No problem. Love you." We both watched him go. If Olive noticed my interest, she didn't comment.

A thought struck me as the bell over the door signaled Sam's departure. "Does he know? About your gifts?"

She shook her head. "He knows I'm quite good at finding a home for used objects, both because the store has always done well and because he used to work here on the weekends in high school. Otherwise, no. My wife knows, but no one else. You know how it is. You don't want people to think less of you. Especially not people with the power to lock you up in a nursing home."

Heh. "You might be old enough to be my mother, but you're a good thirty years away from the nursing home."

"Flattery will get you everywhere. Tell you what. It's been a strange morning. Let me show you around."

I told Olive we had a deal.

For the next couple of hours, we explored the shop, peering into various nooks and crannies. It all looked like a mess, but underneath the chaos lay an organizational system I respected. It might take time to learn it, but after a few weeks, I should be able to find things for customers fairly easily, just like Olive.

Okay, not exactly the same. But the more time I spent here, the more it felt right. Missing Pieces had a homey feel, an aura that helped me feel at peace. I didn't know why, but

I belonged here. By the time we finished the tour and she'd explained how the shop operated, I was excited about my new job.

"Can you start tomorrow?"

"I've got Kyle in the morning," I said. "His school is closed for teacher meetings. But I can be here after lunch."

"Deal."

We were just finishing negotiating my hours and pay when the bell jingled behind me. Cold wind rushed through the open door, swirling around the store. Footsteps thudded across the threshold.

A voice rang out. "Olive Green, you charlatan! Where are you?"

4

Although my first inclination should have been to see who stood at the front of the store screaming, my brain instead fixated on the man's words. "Green? Your name is Olive *Green*? Did your parents not like you?"

"Very funny. You're the first person to say that. Green is my married name." She turned away to face the newcomer before shooting over her shoulder, "And you're one to talk, Aluminum."

Touché.

The man stormed into the room, then stopped dead at the sight of me. He looked vaguely familiar. That could be a Shady Grove thing: you tended to cross paths with pretty much everyone at some point. He was medium height, built like a refrigerator, bald, with a vein the size of New Mexico throbbing in his forehead. His dark eyes flashed beneath bushy grey eyebrows, and red splotches were working their way up his cheeks.

"How can I help you, Earl?" Olive moved behind the counter, both giving her an air of authority and creating a physical barrier between her and the man. Smart. I wondered if she kept a panic button back there.

"You can give me my money back, that's how!" He slammed something onto the counter with such force, I jumped. "This darn trinket is no good! You sold me cheap junk."

Olive shook her head. "Look, Earl, I told you there were no guarantees. Love is a tricky business. You can't rely on trinkets. You need to use your wit and charm to win someone over. I can't help it if you don't have either of those things."

His face turned purple. "Listen up woman, I'll call the town council if I have to!"

"And tell them what? That you set your sights on some pretty young thing who refused to sleep with you, even after you tried to invoke the great roofie spirit? Come on, Earl."

"I'll have you know that I have no problem getting women to sleep with me, thank you very much."

As badly as I wanted to point out that if his love life were fine, he wouldn't be standing in the store screaming at us about a love goddess that didn't work, my more rational side reined me in. No need to escalate the situation.

"I'm not a witch. And even if I were, I wouldn't do love spells. You want a conduit, go to the magic shop. This is a trinket. I never made you any promises," Olive said. "Sorry, but I don't offer refunds. You know that. It's on your receipt."

Helpfully, I pointed at a three-foot square sign with four-inch red letters hanging on the wall behind her left shoulder. "It's also right there."

Earl turned to glare at me. "Who are you?"

"Aly is my new employee, and you'll be kind to her or get out," Olive said. "On second thought, just get out. We can't help you."

"I'm not leaving until I get my money."

"Well, then, you'll get hungry later," she said. "I'm closing up at six and going home, like I do every weeknight."

I shifted uneasily from one foot to the other. Her mention of time reminded me that Kevin expected me to pick Kyle up from school at three, and I still needed to buy groceries to help him make dinner. Even though he was only three, my nephew adored cooking. At this rate, he'd be winning *MasterChef Junior* before I finished my college degree.

Between the ring fiasco and our angry customer, I'd completely lost track of time. I was going to be very late. Not knowing what else to do, I cleared my throat awkwardly.

"What's wrong, dear?" Olive asked. "Don't let this old goat bother you."

"Old goat? I'm three months younger than your wife!" Earl bellowed.

"I'm so sorry, but I have to pick up my nephew. I don't want to leave you here like this. Can Sam come back?"

"Sam's probably halfway home by now." She waved one hand. "It's fine, dear. I'll see you in the morning."

Earl was still ranting and raving when the door swung shut behind me. It didn't feel right to leave her alone, but I reminded myself that Olive took care of herself just fine before I came along. The issue became moot seconds later when the bell jingled again, and Earl stormed past me.

I shrank into the shadows, but he either didn't see me or didn't care. A moment later, he slammed the door of a shiny red convertible. The engine roared. As the car zoomed out of sight, I caught a glimpse of the license plate: HAWTSTF.

Hot stuff? Someone had a high opinion of himself. I rolled my eyes. Why not just say "MIDLIFE" to describe the clear crisis he was having? Ah, well. I had more important things to worry about than an irate customer at a job I hadn't even started yet. It was Wasabi Wednesday, and Kyle waited for me to pick him up so he could help me roll the sushi. Sushi that required rice I still needed to purchase. Along with wasabi and, well, all the other ingredients.

The big supermarket was at least half an hour away in Willow Falls. I wouldn't have time to get there and back, so I swung by the smaller Grocery Mart instead. Who needed real wasabi, anyway?

There was rarely a line at the corner store. Of course, when there was, it always formed behind the town gossip, the only person in the state who still used a checkbook. Luckily, Thelma wasn't around today, or I'd have lost another ten minutes. That probably would've earned me a stern lecture from Mr. Spaulding, the principal, on punctuality. I raced home, dumped the groceries on the kitchen counter, then took off toward the preschool, luckily only two blocks away. As it was, I arrived at pickup with about ninety seconds to spare.

My nephew squinted up at me when I screeched to a halt in front of him, panting. He was tall for his age, and I wasn't, so he already came up practically to my ribcage. His serious brown eyes peered out at me from beneath his red ski cap, which perched precariously atop chestnut curls so like Kevin's and mine. My nephew had inherited his mother's pert nose and heart-shaped lips, but otherwise he was all Reynolds.

"Why is your face red?" Kyle asked.

"I'm excited to see you!" And also, I might be dying. A stitch in my side made breathing impossible.

The teacher's aide eyed me but didn't comment. Kyle turned to him. "Mark, am I face red?"

"No."

"Why not, Aunt Aly? I excited."

"I've been outside longer." This was true, and a much better answer. Probably the one I should've given in the first place. I braced myself for the request for a scientific explanation, which came about forty percent of the time.

Apparently today was my lucky day, because my nephew switched over to talking about the "jumping box" in his classroom, where he could stand and jump as long as he wanted. I got very nervous about this concept until Mark assured me that it was just duct tape arranged in a square on the floor.

The afternoon passed in the usual flurry of activity, getting Kyle his snack while listening to him talk about his day, practicing his reading, and cooking dinner.

After we ate, Kevin went to his weekly bowling league while Kyle and I raced toy cars until bedtime. Finally, after two requests for water, three trips to the bathroom, and four stories, I hugged my delightful nephew and said goodnight.

"G'Night," he said. "I happy you got a job."

"Thanks, buddy. Me, too."

I stood in the doorway for a long moment before I shut the door, thinking about the turn my life had taken in the past year. Before Katrina died, I'd been going to school, taking labs, and working in the campus bookstore. Most of my free time was spent with my BFF and roommate, Carly.

We had the kind of friendship borne of having last names adjacent in the alphabet and therefore spending fifteen years sitting next to each other in school. Our junior year, poor Juan Rodriguez transferred in and got stuck between Aly Reynolds and Carly Rogers. He spent half the year listening to us talk around him in the moments before class. Then he asked Carly out, and they started whispering without me. Not that it mattered. That was the year I discovered the *Hitchhiker's Guide* books and started secretly reading under my desk whenever I had a spare minute. Since I tended to finish my work pretty fast, that was often.

Anyway, three years ago, we'd moved into our first apartment together. I was getting an associate's degree in biology while Carly studied art history. We both cried when I moved to Shady Grove. Now she worked at a local museum, organizing events and having the time of her life while she went to school at night to finish her last few credits. Meanwhile, I just applied for a job working for a woman who thought she was psychic.

Even more hilariously, Olive thought I was psychic. Which reminded me: I had research to do before Kevin got home.

I blew Kyle one last kiss goodnight and went downstairs to make coffee. This could take a while. Researching hallucinogenic metals wasn't exactly as easy as singing A-B-Cs with a three-year-old. Nor was it nearly as cute.

After settling onto the couch, I got to work. I needed as much information as possible before showing up at work tomorrow morning.

Unfortunately, I didn't have the first clue where to start. My college-level biology classes didn't spend much time talking about psychics. My research didn't bring up any liquid hallucinogens likely to work in seconds. Unless it wasn't the ring? Maybe there was something in the air. That seemed unlikely, though, since Olive, Sam, and Earl were all in the store, too. Unless the same substance caused my vision and Earl's rage, that theory was a non-starter.

If I had kept the ring, it might be possible to test the metal for various acids or other substances. Unfortunately, despite Olive's insisting that I take it, I'd left it in the store "accidentally." I never wanted to touch it again. It didn't matter that Olive thought the ring belonged to me. She could sell it to anyone else.

When I was ready to start banging my head against the desk, my mind turned to something else Olive mentioned during our interview: my sister-in-law. What happened to the investigation into Katrina's death? That whole time blurred together in my mind. So many things happened at once. Kev was distraught, Kyle was confused and sad. A police officer at the funeral ask a few questions I couldn't answer because I'd been in California. As far as I knew, the case had been open ever since. Kev would have told me if they'd caught someone, but did that mean we'd never know who did it?

With a glance over my shoulder to ensure Kyle was still sleeping—as if he could get out of his room without me knowing it—I opened a new tab and typed "Katrina Reynolds death" into the search bar. A clipping from the paper in the fancy suburb where they'd lived popped up at the top, as well as a pretty standard obit by the funeral home that handled the ceremony.

The page contained all the basics: name, age, loving wife, loving mother. She had a sister, who I didn't remember from the funeral. That was it. Not a peep about what happened to her, just a note that she "left this world all too soon." I sighed and rubbed my eyes. What did I hope to find, anyway? A random clue in a photograph that would resolve everything? That sounded like a great movie plot, but this was real life.

Back to psychics. So far, all of my research revolved around whether they were frauds. But after a moment's thought, I decided to expand my hypothesis. What if psychics were real? What would the signs be? How might a person find out if they were one? Hundreds of pages of results popped up.

Element eight is oxygen. O.

Oh, man, this could take forever.

Page after page filled the screen, but I didn't find anything conclusive. As Olive hinted earlier, apparently psychic gifts took many forms. No one sold a how-to manual. The whole thing hurt my brain.

When I got tired of reading, I gave myself a break. Olive wasn't the only fascinating person I'd met today. Opening yet another a new tab, I typed "Sam Green." Not shockingly, I got about forty million results. A dead end. Back at the top, I typed "Olive Green Shady Grove" which got me pages both for her and Missing Pieces. From her profile, I went to "relationships" and there he was. Sam Green, Son. As absolutely beautiful on the screen as he'd been in person.

His profile picture showed him alone, which gave me hope. No relationship status. I'd been hoping for single, but at least it didn't show him with someone else. Then again, he posted almost nothing on Facebook. Either his profile was closed down to non-friends or he didn't use it much. Probably both. I couldn't send him a friend request since I didn't use Facebook. Creating a profile just to talk to a man I'd met for about four minutes seemed excessive. Instead I moved over to Instagram.

By the time the outer garage door rumbled upward, I was no closer to figuring out what had happened to me, but I'd ogled about twenty images of Sam and discovered that he'd arrived safely home in Brooklyn in time to make it to his friend's World Record attempt. The event itself was apparently still going strong, expected to take all night. The National Museum of Mathematics had posted about four hundred pictures, and I combed through all of them.

Because I'm fascinated by numbers, not to see if Sam brought a date to the event. (Good news! He appeared to be with a group of friends.)

As much fun as that was, it wasn't remotely informative. Google couldn't answer the types of questions that had been going through my head all day. Like it or not, I needed Olive. I heaved a sigh. It was time for bed once I said good-night to Kevin, and I was no closer to figuring things out now than at three o'clock this afternoon.

Outside, the garage door slid into place. The interior door to the mudroom squeaked open, something we'd been meaning to fix. Then my brother walked into view, and all thoughts of magical rings fled. Kevin looked like he'd gotten hit by a bus.

It hadn't been uncommon to see him falling down with exhaustion when I first moved here, but over the past few months, we'd settled into our routine. He began sleeping better, the bags beneath his brown eyes vanished, and he started laughing and smiling more. He actually started looking his age instead of ten years older. An amazing transformation.

But now, all that progress had been erased. He looked as hollow-eyed as the day I'd arrived. He kept his hair short to keep the curls so like Kyle's under control, but the locks stuck out as if he'd spent the last twenty minutes running his hands through it.

"Kevin? What's wrong? Are Mom and Dad okay?"

He nodded slowly, walking toward the couch like a zombie before he bent his knees just enough to perch on the edge of the cushions. He lowered his head into his hands, staring at the floor.

I went to my brother and sat beside him, rubbing his back. "You're starting to scare me."

"Sorry, Aly. Mom and Dad are fine, last I heard. I haven't talked to them in a few days. But I'm sure they're fine."

Okay, that was good. And yet, if not something with our parents, and knowing Kyle was upstairs asleep in bed, I couldn't imagine anything terrible enough to put that look on Kevin's face. "What happened?"

"There's been a murder." He sighed. "Earl Parker is dead."

5

I gaped at my brother in disbelief. Earl was dead? The same guy who had a verbal coronary in Missing Pieces only a few hours earlier? He was only like fifty.

Okay, I knew people could die at any age. Katrina proved that. But still. It was so weird. I couldn't wrap my head around the idea that someone who stood in front of me a few hours ago was not only dead, but had been murdered. Shady Grove wasn't Los Angeles or Boston or even Albany. People didn't get murdered here. That's one of the reasons Kevin picked this town in the first place—low crime, lower murder. Only one person named after a scientific unit of temperature.

Mentally, I shook myself. My mind went weird places when I got stressed. Element nine is fluorine. F.

F was right.

A strangled sound escaped me. The words didn't compute. I didn't know what to think, what to say.

"Are you okay?" Kevin asked. "I didn't realize you even knew Earl."

"I didn't," I said. "Not really. I met him this afternoon.

But also, like, I *saw* him this afternoon. He was walking and talking and breathing. He seemed so alive." Also throwing a fit, but that didn't seem worth mentioning. "How do you know him?"

"He's in my bowling league," Kevin said. Ah. Well, that at least explained why Earl had looked familiar. A couple of times when Kevin had Saturday afternoon races or meets or whatever they're called, I'd brought Kyle to the bowling alley to run around the arcade. "Or at least, he was. Best in the league. Now that honor goes to Wendy Diaz. She bowled eleven perfect games last year, but then her Pit Bull, Fluffykins, got sick. She missed the finals. You must remember me talking about it."

So much information in that one paragraph. My brother's head must be spinning as much as mine. Probably more, since he had a relationship with the guy. "What happened?"

"Too much grass, maybe. Or spending all day outside in the sun. I'm not sure."

That made no sense at all. Earl died from eating grass in the sun in January? Then I realized, Kevin thought I was asking about the dog.

"Yeah, okay. But also, what happened to Earl?"

"No one knows," he said. "Every Wednesday, he eats lunch at Patti's Diner. He orders the same thing, always tips fifteen percent rounded up. When he finishes lunch, he usually lingers, but Patti said he left early today to run an errand. She didn't know what it was."

"You already talked to Patti? When did you leave the bowling alley?"

"She was there. Patti's in my league. You'd know that if you ever came with me."

"If I came with you, you'd need to pay for a babysitter.

Plus all the toes I'd break because I don't know how to bowl. Tell me more."

"I don't know much else," he said. "He was supposed to have dinner with his next-door neighbor, Thelma. Apparently they do that a few times a week. He didn't show up, so she went looking for him. She knocked, then noticed the kitchen door was ajar."

"Did she run as fast as possible in the other direction? Because that's what a smart person would do." Or anyone who had ever watched a horror movie.

Kevin chuckled. "Not Thelma. She claims she just snuck a peek, but if I know her, she probably banged the door open and waltzed in shouting his name. No matter, the killer was gone. She found Earl slumped over the kitchen table. Blood everywhere."

One hand went to my mouth. The primary reason I changed my major from pre-med to biology was a strong aversion to blood. Like, I watched horror movies peeking through my fingers. Tending Kyle's scrapes nauseated me. Graphic descriptions of death scenes were way beyond my comfort zone. Even though I'd never met Thelma, I felt bad for her. No one deserved to stumble onto a crime scene while preparing to serve dinner.

"Oh, no. That's horrible. Can you imagine what it would be like to find someone you love de—." In horror, I realized what I'd been about to say. My brother didn't have to imagine, because it happened to him. Only it wasn't his neighbor, it was his wife, and her killer was still out there. "Oh, Kev. I'm sorry. I wasn't thinking."

"I know." He closed his eyes for a long moment. "It's fine. Let's go to bed."

There was nothing else to say, so I put my arm around him and let him lean against my shoulder. When he pulled away, I turned toward the stairs. "What do you need right now?"

"I'll be fine," he said. "Just some rest. It's been a long day."

A long day indeed. I barely managed to brush my teeth and climb into bed before falling asleep.

Next thing I knew, my bedroom door swung open, and a small torpedo landed on the comforter beside me. "Aunt Aly!"

"'Mmmph." I wrapped my arms around Kyle's tiny neck while glaring at my brother in the doorway. "Isn't it your turn to get him up?"

Kevin laughed. "That I did. An hour ago."

"We made waffles!"

Waffles? I looked at my brother for confirmation.

"To celebrate your new job. I also made coffee."

Coffee. Yeeeeesssss. I pushed up and swung my legs over the side of the bed.

"Hug!" Kyle demanded from his spot beside me.

How could anyone say no to those big eyes asking for a hug in that tiny voice? I reached for him, and he leaned into me. Most people hugged with their arms, but Kyle hugged with his whole heart. Toddler snuggles were absolutely the best thing in the world.

Five minutes later, we finally made it downstairs. To my delight there really was a pile of fresh waffles and a pot of coffee sitting on the kitchen table. "Oh, this is wonderful! You shouldn't have."

"I didn't," Kevin said proudly. "This is all Kyle. He planned the whole thing."

"You made me waffles?"

Kyle beamed up at me. "Daddy ironed them."

The phrasing made me chuckle. "Daddy's a good helper, isn't he?"

"Not as good as you," Kevin said behind me. "Seriously. We wanted you to know how much we appreciate you. You've done so much for us."

I gave him an awkward one-armed hug. "I did what anyone would've. We're family."

Once we were all seated, I forked a huge bite of waffles into my mouth. My eyes closed blissfully. "Oh, wow."

This kid was so talented. I didn't even have to pretend to enjoy the meal. For several minutes, we focused on our breakfasts. Normally I ate a piece of toast or two slathered with Nutella, so strawberry waffles with whipped cream were quite the treat.

When our plates were so clean they might've been licked (and, okay, Kyle's definitely had been), Kevin excused himself to go upstairs. He'd been quiet throughout the meal, and I knew Earl's death weighed heavily on his mind. I watched him go, wondering how things might be different if Katrina were still alive.

I'd probably be in Sacramento, living with Gabby, about to start my final semester of classes. Would I have had a vision yesterday, while out at a bar celebrating my birthday?

My nephew looked at me seriously over his waffles. "You look sad."

I leaned over and ruffled his hair. "Everything's fine. I'm thinking about how much I'm going to miss you when you're at school and I'm at work."

"Work is good for the soul," he announced. "Daddy said."

I laughed and slung back the rest of my coffee. "Sounds like your father. That man loves what he does. Let's get going."

Kyle's preschool was closed for teacher training, so I'd planned to visit the campus bookstore. Maloney College wasn't the most obvious destination for a niece-nephew outing in late January, but I needed to familiarize myself with the layout before classes started. Also, I'd learned the hard way that I preferred to page through used books before committing. My first year of community college, someone had made pornographic sketches in the margins of my Calculus book. Still didn't make math sexy. And my geology book? Every single word was highlighted.

Dude, if it's all important, none of it is important. I saw yellow spots every time I closed my eyes for three months.

The bookstore sat on the edge of campus, next to the gym and not far from the history building. According to the map on Maloney's website, the science building was at the end of the path, which wound around for about a mile.

I hesitated before pulling Kyle out of his car seat. "Do you want to ride in the stroller?"

He glared at me. "I'm not a baby!"

"True, but it's a lot of walking. You might get tired."

"I walk."

To be honest, I had my doubts, but we'd be starting at the bookstore. Since I had no intention of lugging my purchases all over campus, I could always grab the stroller when I came back to drop them off. Sometimes it wasn't worth arguing with a three-year-old.

I set him on the ground to get him into the coat he couldn't wear while strapped into his car seat. Some days, I swore I would dedicate my post-college studies to making a jacket that toddlers could wear in the car. Or a car seat with effectiveness that wasn't reduced by clothing necessary in huge portions of the country for several months each year.

Kyle lunged away from me. "Ball!"

What?

Oh. Across the aisle, a guy about my age was struggling to load an arm full of stuff into his trunk. A basketball thudded to the pavement and rolled toward us. Kyle took three steps toward it before I caught him. "Stop! We have to look both ways, remember?"

My nephew pointed. "Ball?"

"That's right. It's his ball. That guy. Not ours."

The guy in question turned and smiled at me as the ball rolled close enough for Kyle to grab it. He picked it up and turned it in his hands for a moment before chucking it down the road. "Uh-oh!"

I stifled a laugh as it sailed by the owner. He put his hands on his hips and shook his head with a bemused smile that widened when he turned to me. His brown eyes sparkled with laughter, and... he was wearing shorts and a tank top. In January. In upstate New York.

"Aren't you cold?" I blurted out, completely forgetting about the ball. Kyle ran after it a second time. Now that I could see there weren't any other cars, I let him. "Sorry. That was rude."

"No, it's cool. I was just practicing," he said. "I'm on the basketball team, and we've got a big game next week."

The ball sailed by us a second time, now flying in the opposite direction. Life with a toddler led to some very disjointed adult conversations. I motioned for Kyle to come back to me and, thankfully, he did it. There was always like a seventy-seven percent chance he'd do whatever he wanted.

"Stay with me." To the guy, I said, "Sorry about that. We'll get it."

"It's fine," he said. "I've been chasing balls all day. What's one more?"

"Consider it a cool down."

"Just what I needed." Now this was the life. Chatting with random guys in parking lots, buying books, exploring campus. Not a murderer in sight. This was what I wanted— a normal life. Not visions and dead bodies. "I'm Brad."

"Aly. This is my nephew, Kyle."

"You a student here?"

"Not yet. I'm starting midterm."

He motioned to the car. "Sweet ride."

"Thanks," I said. "I couldn't afford a car like this in a million years. It belongs to my brother."

Beside me, my nephew tugged at my hand, clearly tired of this conversation. "I go poop!"

"Okay, one minute." To Brad, I said, "Sorry, we've got to find a bathroom. It's a long drive from Shady Grove."

"You're from Shady Grove? You guys hear about the murder?"

Yes. Not that I wanted to talk about it in front of a three-year-old.

"What's murda, Aunt Aly?"

Awesome. Thanks, Brad. "It's a word for when something bad happens to someone."

On that note, it was time to get going. So much for avoiding thoughts about death this morning. I gripped Kyle's hand and turned toward the bookstore. "It was nice meeting you, Brad."

"You, too. Maybe I'll see you around."

In my experience, the science nerds and the jocks didn't spend much time together, but it was a nice thought. "Sure. Maybe."

Kyle had been standing still long enough. He trotted beside me down the path, up the steps to the library's entrance. Thankfully, the restroom was near the front doors. I didn't want to carry my nephew all over the building while he desperately tried not to poop on me. Potty training was so much fun.

Fifteen minutes later, we'd finished using the potty, washing our hands, and carefully avoiding the hand dryers. Those things were terrifying for small children. I'd learned the hard way to carry a hand towel in my bag. Two minutes after that, we made it to the rows of science textbooks. I ran my finger lovingly along the shelves, feeling right at home among all the multi-syllable words. Going back to school had been the right decision.

After a moment, I bent down to pull a used Molecular Biology textbook that didn't look too battered. For a long moment, I tested the weight in my hands before holding the binding to my nose and taking a deep breath. Ahh.

Don't get me wrong. I loved Kevin, I loved Kyle, and Shady Grove was a nice place. But being here felt like coming home. I missed school, I missed learning. I missed that feeling of being exactly where I was supposed to be, doing exactly what I was supposed to do.

My old life beckoned, and more than anything, I wanted to slide back into it. A life of facts and experiments and no one pooping on me and no visions.

Opening the book, I flipped through the pages, looking for inappropriate markings or excessive highlights. The words swam.

Pulsing lights filled my vision. Music pounded in my ears. A line of white powder lay on the open book in front of me.

6

A shriek escaped me. I dropped the book, jumping backward. As soon as it hit the ground, the world went back to normal. My body still shook, though. What was going on?

I seriously needed to figure out what was happening to me, fast. I couldn't go through life worried that anything I touched might send me a random vision. Was the book trying to tell me something? Who owned it? Did they need my help?

"Are you okay?" An amused voice spoke from behind me. "I know some people hate my class, but I've never seen anyone throw the book before."

Turning, I spotted a woman in her late forties. She had shoulder-length blonde hair, a long, pointed nose, and full lips that twitched as if she was trying not to laugh.

"Your book?"

"I'm Professor Tabitha Zimm. I'm teaching Molecular Biology and Cellular Biology this spring." As she tucked a lock of hair behind one ear, I noticed her long, bubble-gum pink fingernails, cut into perfect squares with hearts on them. Not what you'd expect from a college professor, but I liked people who surprised me.

"Oh!" A smile spread across my face. "It's great to meet you! I'm Aly Reynolds. I mean, the roll sheet will say Aluminum, but please never, ever call me that. I'm so excited about your class. The book... um... startled me."

Beside me, Kyle picked up the book and handed it back to me. "Book?"

"Thanks, sweetie." No chance of me buying that one. Awkwardly, I put it on the shelf before grabbing a pristine new copy. It cost three times more, but if it came without the side of partying, I'd suck it up and ask Olive for some extra hours at the store.

She squinted toward us. "Hello! Who are you?"

"This is my nephew, Kyle."

"I love your shirt! Is that a dog?"

He gave her a withering look. "It's Elmo."

"Shh! Be polite," I said.

Professor Zimm's face turned red as she spoke to me again. "Sorry. I misplaced my glasses earlier. I can barely see."

"Murda glasses?"

If I ever saw Brad again, I was going to kick him in the knees for that one. To her credit, Professor Zimm seemed unfazed. "No, I didn't murder my glasses. I'm sure I'll find them."

Reaching out, Kyle touched her hand. He gazed up at my professor solemnly. "Potty."

"Do you need to go to the bathroom again?" I asked.

He shook his head and pointed at the professor. "Glasses. Potty."

Okay, this was getting weird. Time to take the three-year-old home. Maybe with a stop for Happy Meals and a talk about words that should never, ever be repeated.

"Huh. You know, I was in the restroom earlier. You don't think...?" Professor Zimm spoke slowly.

"We just came from there. It's possible Kyle saw a pair of glasses on the counter." I didn't notice anything, but I was also juggling a portable potty seat and Post-It notes and extra pants and underwear, whereas my nephew didn't have to focus on much other than leaning forward so he didn't paint the back of the stall door with urine.

"I'll go check. It was nice meeting you," she said.

"You, too. I'll see you in class."

"Did I murda your tee-cha?" Kyle asked as she walked away.

I sighed and shook my head. People said small-town life wasn't interesting, but Shady Grove certainly never bored me. We wrapped up my shopping quickly, and I decided to save the rest of my explorations for another day.

Two hours later, after leaving Kyle with Mrs. Patel, I once again stood outside the front door of Missing Pieces. The Help Wanted sign had vanished, but everything else looked the same. The whole town looked the same. Not like the first murder in two decades happened less than twelve hours ago (a fact I'd discovered using my phone this morning over breakfast).

Inside, Olive looked well-rested and full of life. I eyed her for a moment before carefully asking how she was feeling. Maybe she hadn't heard the news.

"Oh, I slept like a baby," she said. "Took a pill after Maria told me what happened to Earl. Went out like a light."

"Maria?"

"My wife."

Right. Olive mentioned yesterday that she was married. "How did she find out?"

"She's on Earl's bowling team. When he didn't show up to practice, people started to talk. He didn't answer his phone, so she called Thelma to see if everything was okay."

Did the entire town hang out at We All Fall Down after work? Was I missing out by not being there? I filed that away under "Things to Ask About When Bored Enough to Want to Learn to Bowl." Group sports weren't my thing. Neither was being coordinated or leaving the house when I didn't have to, especially in winter.

Between learning the inventory and going over the store policies, the afternoon flew by. We had steady business, but not so much I couldn't get time to breathe. Before I knew it, the grandfather clocked chimed four o'clock. The store had cleared out briefly, but the floor near the door was a mess of salt and sludge from all the traffic we'd gotten. I grabbed a mop and a "Wet Floor" sign and went to fix it.

"When you finish that, why don't you take a break? We've been busy."

"Thanks," I said gratefully. As badly as I wanted to tell her to go first, I was tired and hadn't had time for lunch after dropping Kyle off with the sitter. I could really use a sandwich and a few minutes to myself. I hadn't even told Olive yet what happened at the university bookstore.

A moment later, the floor shone, even if I did say so myself. I was about to leave when the bells over the door rang, and a police officer walked into the room, stomping snow and ice off his boots onto the mat.

The officer approached the front counter. His baby face surprised me. Police always seemed like real adults, the kind of adulty adults who were in their forties, at least. But this guy looked only a couple of years older than me. Of course, you didn't need a college degree to join the police force.

I struggled to keep my voice steady. "Good afternoon. Can I help you?"

"I hope so. I'm Doug Matthews."

"You're Sheriff Matthews?" My eyes widened. I swept my gaze from his close-cropped black hair to his wide smile and the adorable cleft in his chin. I'd never met a hot sheriff before, at least not outside of the movies.

"What, you've never seen a Black police officer?"

I rolled my eyes at him. "No, not at all. I'm surprised because—" *you're really hot.* I couldn't say it. I couldn't let him think I believed Black men couldn't be sheriff. Finally, I went with, "You're so young. You're practically my age."

"I'm twenty-seven," he said proudly. "And no. Sheriff *Timothy* Matthews is my uncle. Based on your surprise, I'm guessing you didn't vote for him."

I shrugged. "The last election was before I moved here. How can I help you, Officer?"

"Please, call me Doug," he said. "I'm here to talk to Olive."

"Sure. Why?"

"I'm afraid that's classified."

About Earl. Someone must've told him about their argument. There was no other reason for police to show up. Before I could think, I blurted out, "Earl was alive when he left yesterday!"

"Well, yes, I assumed so," Doug said. "Considering that he wasn't in the store when we found him. Do you know where he went after he left?"

"No, but he drove south on Main. While I was walking home, I saw him."

Doug pulled out a tape recorder. "Do you mind if I record our conversation?"

"Uh, sure?" He gave me a puzzled look. "I mean, no, I don't mind. But I don't know anything. I only met Earl once, for less than five minutes."

"Anything you can tell me will help with the investigation." He put the recorder on the counter, then pressed a button.

When he motioned for me to continue, I went over everything that happened. How I'd been in the store interviewing for a job when Earl tried to return a statuette, and Olive told him there were no refunds. He was angry, she was calm. No reason to think she was upset with him. I'd left, and he'd stormed past me on the sidewalk. Then he got in his car and zoomed away, out of sight.

"Like I said, I don't know much."

"You know more than you think," Doug said. "The timing suggests that, other than the murderer, you may have been the last person to see Earl alive."

A shiver went down my spine at Doug's pronouncement.

It shouldn't bother me. There was absolutely zero connection between me seeing Earl shortly before he died and his getting killed. But it still weirded me out.

"What was he wearing?" Doug asked.

I blinked at him several times. I had no idea. Unless someone showed up in something really unusual like Olive's Civil War-era dress or his uniform, I rarely noticed clothes. In fact, I probably couldn't tell him what I was wearing without looking down first.

"Sorry. I don't know. Is his outfit a clue?"

"Maybe." He shrugged. "If he changed clothes."

"Can you tell me what happened?" I asked. "All I know is

that Thelma found Earl, and they were supposed to have dinner."

"Obviously, any information related to the investigation is confidential."

"Right. I knew that." Of course he wouldn't tell me anything. Not only was I a random stranger to him, I was the last person to see the murder victim alive *and* I worked for the woman who had a loud argument with him only a few hours earlier. Now that I thought about it, I was lucky Doug hadn't slapped handcuffs on me yet.

"But Thelma has been broadcasting her story all over town," he said. "I suppose there's no harm in telling you that her official statement was posted in this morning's Globe."

"In the newspaper? Is that normal?"

"No. No, it's not. We prefer our key witnesses talk to police before the media. Articles usually come from speaking to a source at the police station—here, that's me or Uncle Tim. However, Thelma was on the phone with the press when we arrived on scene." He shook his head in a "what are you gonna do?" gesture.

"I don't want you to get into any trouble, Officer," I said. "Why don't I go get Olive for you, and I'll read the *Globe* while the two of you chat?"

"Sounds great."

Five minutes later, my boss explained to Doug how Earl tossed the figurine at her head while I settled into the nearby table, holding up the morning paper as if I wasn't avidly listening to every word. I wanted to actually read the story at some point, but this conversation was more important.

"Why didn't you call the police?" Doug asked. "That's assault."

Olive shrugged. "He missed."

"But still."

"Look, if Earl had come any closer, I'd have walloped him. But he threw the statuette, I ducked, he left. That's the end of it."

Under his breath, the officer muttered something that sounded suspiciously like, "Would have walloped him."

Olive wasn't helping her own case. Maybe I should call Kevin. He didn't practice criminal law, but at the very least, he could advise Olive not to tell police that she'd thought about "walloping" the guy who later died of a head injury. Even I knew that. Hoping I looked casual, I picked up my phone and tapped out a text.

Moments later, the store phone rang.

"Excuse me, sweetie," Olive said. "I need to take this. Missing Pieces, how can I help you?"

She listened and nodded for about thirty seconds before putting the receiver back into the cradle. Then she shot me a look I couldn't read before turning to Doug. "I've been advised by my attorney not to answer any further questions without him present."

Doug narrowed his eyes at me but directed his comments at Olive. "Oh, yeah? What a coincidence. Your lawyer?"

"Yes. I am now represented by Kevin Reynolds, Esquire."

He slid his gaze over to me and placed his hand on his heart. "Aly, you wound me. I thought we were becoming friends."

"You're cute, Doug, but not that cute," I said. "Don't you have a murderer to catch?"

"I suppose that's my cue to leave. But I'll be back." The words hovered in the air ominously. A moment later the bells jingled as the door swung shut behind him.

As soon as the ringing stopped, Olive turned to me,

hands on her hips. "Just what do you think you're doing, missy?"

I stood up, mirroring her posture. "Don't missy me! I'm saving you. You practically told the police that you thought about attacking Earl. Why not post 'I've got a motive!' on a billboard?"

"You obviously didn't know Earl," she muttered. "Half the town had a motive to kill him."

"Those comments aren't helping your case."

"My case doesn't need help. I'm not a killer."

"You know that, and I know that," I said with a glance at the closed door. "But we may need to convince the rest of the town. You practically gave a confession."

"I did no such thing!" Her features softened, though. "But thank you for looking out for me. I've known Doug Matthews since he was in diapers."

"Everyone's known everyone for years around here. No one thinks their friends and neighbors are capable of murder. And yet, someone had to do it."

She sighed. "True enough. What does the paper say?"

According to the front page, Earl worked as a gardener in the summer, snowplow driver in the winter. This time of year, he worked before dawn to make sure his customers could get out of their driveways when they woke up. Since it snowed late Tuesday night, he'd been working early on the day he died. He'd finished his normal rounds, but only one of the homeowners saw him. She didn't notice anything out of the ordinary. That wasn't too helpful.

I didn't know why I hoped it would be. It's not like he'd show up to plow her driveway with "LATER I'M GOING TO BE MURDERED BY THIS PERSON" painted on the back of his truck.

Earl ate lunch at Patti's Diner, which was also no

surprise since it was one of only two restaurants around and the other didn't serve lunch. Also because Kevin had already told me. No one saw Earl again until he turned up at Missing Pieces. He left here a few minutes later, presumably driving home. If he stopped, no one had yet reported seeing him. (Or they were smart enough not to tell the *Globe*.) Thelma found him a couple of hours later, dead.

Not much to go on.

"Have you talked to anyone else about this?" I asked Olive.

"Just Maria. And we called Sam last night. Why?"

"I'm wondering if we were his only stop on Main Street. Maybe he went somewhere else before he came here. Someone else might know something."

She shrugged. "I suppose it's possible. A lot of businesses shut down over the past year, but there are a few places he might have gone."

My boss seemed completely unconcerned at the prospect of police thinking she may have killed someone. I didn't know how to help her understand the severity of the situation. Hopefully Kevin could talk some sense into her. But I knew one thing: I needed to get to the bottom of this.

If Olive went to jail, I would never find out about my gifts or how to use them properly. I didn't really know what was happening to me, but I didn't want to lose my only chance to find out.

7

"We have to find out who did killed Earl," I said with more confidence than I felt.

"What? Why on earth would we get involved in finding a killer?" Olive asked. "Leave that to the professionals."

"Did you hear anything Officer Matthews said? Right now, you're their most likely suspect."

"That's absurd! Lots of people probably wanted to kill Earl."

Hmmm. Not exactly a fervent denial. Not that I really thought she was guilty, but... "Did you do it?"

Her eyes widened. "How can you even ask me that?"

I shrugged. "I mean, I don't think you did. But I just met you, and in science, the best course of action is to form a hypothesis and then test to eliminate possibilities."

"So your hypothesis is that I killed Earl?" Under her breath, Olive muttered, "You're lucky you're gifted, Kid. I need you."

"No," I said patiently. "My hypothesis is that *someone* killed Earl. I know it wasn't me."

"Well, it wasn't me, either," she snapped.

"I believe you. So, in a town of ten thousand people, we've eliminated two."

"Is this your master plan? Walk around town and ask everyone if they've killed Earl until someone says yes?"

"I don't have a plan," I said. "I'm twenty-one. I haven't finished college yet. It's my first full day of work in an antique store. I thought I'd learn to use the cash register, not investigate a murder."

Her face softened. "I'm sorry. Of course not. I'm all out of sorts today. I've known Earl for more than twenty years. I went to high school with his younger brother."

"I'm sorry, I didn't know."

"Thanks. It's just unsettling."

"What about motive? Who might have wanted Earl dead? Any pending inheritance? A jealous lover or ex? Something like that."

She thought for a minute. "To my knowledge, Earl didn't have any kids or much money, so probably not an inheritance. No recent exes. He's been dating Thelma for years. Thelma's friend Benji has been in love with her since he moved to town. She was never going to notice him while she was dating Earl. Also, Wendy was pissed when her beat her for the bowling championship."

Now we were getting somewhere. "Angry enough to kill him?"

She sighed. "Aly, I don't know. We're talking about people I've known half my life. I don't want to believe any of them could be a killer. But yeah, Wendy was mad. She suspected he made her miss the final game, but there was no way to prove it."

"Okay, thanks. Sorry to push so hard. Having police come in here freaked me out. I just want to help."

"I know. And I do have one idea." Turning away, she

rummaged under the counter for a few minutes before pulling something out and putting it on the counter. A small silver statue of a woman, about four inches tall. She had enormous breasts, a rounded stomach, wide hips, and no facial features at all. I recognized it immediately.

"That's the figurine Earl wanted to exchange yesterday, right?"

"Yeah. He chucked her at me on the way out the door. Luckily, his aim sucks as bad as his personality."

"Possibly not the most helpful thing to say about a murder victim when you're the only suspect."

She tilted her head at me. "Then don't repeat it."

We were getting off track. Now, I was no expert, but to me her animosity toward Earl made it seem an awful lot like she had a motive. "What's that for? Did you want to give it to Officer Matthews?"

Olive shook her head. "The interesting thing here, Aly, isn't that Earl tried to exchange something or even what it is, but what you and I can do when we test it with our gifts."

Thus far, I'd had exactly two visions, neither of them clear. The idea of solving a murder with superpowers sounded great, but I didn't think for a second that I could learn anything of value from rubbing a small plastic statue.

I examined the tiny figurine silently for a moment, trying to think what to say. "She's pretty. Who is she? It's not Aphrodite, right?"

"Right. Oshun. Goddess from the Yoruba religion. Sexuality, fertility, love, beauty, luxury, pleasure, the river, and fresh water."

I quirked an eyebrow at her. "The goddess of fresh water? Maybe Oshun told you she belonged to Earl because he needed a bath, not so he could fall in love."

She snorted. "If she'd told me that, it could have saved all of us some trouble. Come on. See what she can tell you."

My suspicious gaze moved from the statue to Olive, then back. "You first."

"I already tried, early this morning. No dice. Our gifts aren't the same. My power tells me who the true owner of an item is. Oshun told me to sell her to Earl when he came in, and I did."

"Does your power tell you why you should give an item to a specific person?"

"I'm afraid not," she said. "And now that Earl's dead, I don't get anything. It's just a paperweight."

"So that's it? No one else can ever own it?" How sad for the poor object that just wanted a home.

She shrugged. "Maybe, or maybe the right person isn't in my sphere yet. I don't have all the answers. I'll stick Oshun in the back room, and if the right person shows up, she'll let me know."

"Seems like a weird way to sell second-hand stuff."

"I don't question my gifts," she said. "I help people find the pieces that are missing in their lives."

Realization dawned. "Like the store's name."

"Exactly."

"You know, when I saw the sign for the first time, I wondered if you sold puzzles. Then I walked in and saw an antique shop. But now, I realize, you really do solve puzzles. Just no one knows what they are except you."

She beamed at me. "That's a lovely way of looking at it. Take the statue."

"What? Why? I don't need any love or fertility in my life." Especially not fertility, not for at least five years. And a partner.

"Not like that," she said. "Just hold it."

I couldn't think of any way to tell her that I was terrified of her suggestion. "You know, I'm tired. I should probably go get some coffee."

"You're stalling. Take it. We need to see what happens."

"We don't know what happened with that ring. It could've been a fluke."

What about the textbook?, my traitorous brain asked.

"Do you really believe a fluke brought you in here, to me? On the same day my gift told me to expect you."

Weakly, I said, "I want to be a scientist. There has to be a rational explanation for this."

"Ah, that's right. Science explains everything. Well then, let's construct a hypothesis and test it."

She parroted what I'd said earlier. "Well-played. What's your hypothesis?"

"I hypothesize that when you touch this figurine, you'll get a clue about Earl's death."

"Why?"

"Clearly something happened that upset him greatly. Maybe you can see what it was."

Even if she was right, I couldn't imagine calling the local police and telling them I'd solved a murder using my newfound psychic powers. One thing at a time, though. I nodded. "Fine. I'll give it a shot."

"Excellent. Here."

"If I get pregnant, I'm blaming you."

She snorted.

Hesitantly, I held out my hand. Olive placed the small statue in my palm. It was cool to the touch, heavier than I expected. At first glance the figure looked like a cheap trinket, but now I suspected she was made of pewter.

Bracing myself, I closed my eyes and curled my fingers around the tiny goddess.

N othing happened.

The statue sat in my palm, cool and smooth and doing absolutely nothing. Opening my eyes, I uncurled my fingers. "What's she supposed to be doing? Is Oshun supposed to come to life and speak to me?"

I felt like a total fool. Tears of embarrassment prickled at my eyes, but I blinked them away.

My first inclination had been right, after all. Whatever happened with the ring was a fluke, or a joke, or a heat-induced hallucination. Time to put this statue down and go watch Neil deGrasse Tyson on YouTube. Science was real, superpowers were not. I should have listened to my gut in the first place, walked out of here, and never come back.

Except, that wasn't what my gut said. That's what my head told me. My head was afraid of what was happening. Science didn't have explanations for absolutely everything.

"I should go," I said.

"I know you're disappointed, dear, but this is all very new. It takes time."

"How much time? Where's the instruction manual?"

Olive shook her head. "I don't think the gift works like that."

"So how does it work?" The obvious answer, of course, was that it didn't. I was just a normal girl who did normal things like getting a job and helping my brother. Touching this statue wouldn't tell me any more than licking a lamppost.

"I don't know." Olive put her hands on her hips, tilting her head at me. "Maybe you need to *believe* in your gift."

"I didn't believe in it yesterday, and I've had two visions since I met you."

"Fair enough, but those came to you. You didn't call them."

Great. Okay. I could do this. Closing my eyes, I willed myself to believe that this tiny pewter goddess was about to tell me something.

Behind my closed eyes, I saw an image of my associate's degree in biology, still in the envelope it had been mailed in. Unframed, in a box somewhere in Kevin's attic. My subconscious mind was such a jerk. I wondered if Olive was recording this, catching my expressions. My nose itched. The patchouli and rose scents hung heavily in the air today.

A man is dead, a voice said inside my head. *Try harder.*

I wanted answers, really, but I had no idea what to do. I scrunched my nose a few times. I forced myself to picture Earl the last time, tearing down the street in his shiny red sports car. I didn't get any feelings at all from the statue. Zip. Zilch. Maybe the tiniest sheen of frustration, but that could be coming from me as much as Earl's spirit or the figurine or whatever.

In the back of the store, the antique clock ticked off the seconds, growing louder and louder until it reverberated through my entire body. Tick tock. I couldn't hear anything else. Tick tock. I couldn't hear my own thoughts. Tick Tock. This wasn't helping. If I stayed like this, I would lose my mind.

With a frustrated sigh, I opened my eyes. The ticking clock receded as Olive's face came into focus. "I'm sorry, I just don't see anything."

She sighed and took the statuette back. "It's okay. You only discovered your gift yesterday. It can take time to figure out how everything works. Maybe your power isn't what we think, or maybe it'll grow stronger the more you use it. You should gain control at some point, learn how to turn it on and off. The only thing that's certain is that it's not working now. We can try again another time."

"So what do we do now?"

"Now?" She gestured around the room. "I'm going in the back to take a break, make some tea. I'll be back in half an hour or so. Call if you need anything."

As soon as Olive returned, I told her that I'd be taking my break. Then I left Missing Pieces and turned right, toward the hottest spot in town for hearing gossip and getting information.

It made sense to start my fact-finding mission at On What Grounds? because, well, coffee. No one could be expected to solve a murder without a good dose of caffeine. Usually the shop was a bustling hive of activity, and today was no different. The owner, Julie, managed the line with ease, laughing and chatting with each customer without making those who waited impatient. The owner described herself as a "recovering lawyer" who moved to Shady Grove a few years ago and took the coffee shop over from her aunt. Julie was a pretty, blue-eyed blonde who looked a few years older than me, not quite as old as my brother. (Kevin just turned thirty.) She couldn't have been a lawyer long before moving here. Not that it was any of my business. I hadn't even finished college yet.

To Julie's left, Rusty manned the espresso machine. Red rimmed his eyes, an old baseball cap covered his hair, and a couple of times, he swayed when moving cups to the pick-up counter. The guy looked on the verge of collapse. I wanted to go to him, ask if everything was okay, but you didn't mess with people's coffee around here. I needed to wait my turn like everyone else.

Snippets of conversation buzzed around me. Not surprisingly, everyone was talking about Earl. In the middle of the room, Thelma sobbed into a giant handkerchief. About thirty years ago, Thelma was a major soap opera star, and it showed in everything she did. These days, she was widely known as the town gossip.

Someone as uninteresting as me rarely inspired her notice, but we'd met once or twice. She wore such heavy makeup I couldn't even be sure of her skin tone, but her face didn't move when she sobbed. She had sharp hazel eyes and gorgeous auburn hair. She was younger than I would have thought. From what everyone said, she'd been living in this town for so long, I figured she'd be closer to my great-grandma's age. But now that I really looked, she appeared to be in her late fifties or early sixties. Around the same age as Earl.

Was she the one he intended to use the statuette on? Maybe she'd rebuffed his advances, one thing led to another, and she'd hit him to get away. They would've been in the kitchen, surrounded by pots and pans...No, wait. Kevin said they were "practically engaged." Did Thelma know he'd bought a love goddess?

"Hey," Julie said when I got to the front of the line. "How you holding up?"

"I'm okay," I said. "Why?"

"It's just that the town is pretty shaken up since, well..." She nodded to where Thelma loudly blew her nose. The handkerchief fluttered from the force. I made a note not to sit beside her. "...you know."

"Thanks, but I'm fine. I only met Earl once." It seemed prudent not to detail the circumstances of that meeting if she didn't already know. Although I suspected everyone in Shady Grove was aware that Earl had visited Missing Pieces shortly before his death, they might know I'd been there.

"Oh, I thought he and your brother were friends?" Julie asked.

I blinked repeatedly, wondering how she knew that. "I'd say 'friends' is a stretch. They were in the same bowling league. As far as I know, they didn't see each other outside of that. Kevin doesn't get out much."

"Yeah, raising a kid alone must be tough." She flushed. "I mean, obviously, you're helping. I just meant, he must be lonely. Having your kid sister around isn't the same as a spouse."

"We take care of each other," I said evenly, wondering at her interest. Kevin had never mentioned Julie, but he must know her. Not only did he know everyone, but the man loved his midday cappuccinos. "Listen, did you see anything yesterday?"

She shook her head as she swiped my credit card. "No, nothing. Rusty and I were here all day. Yesterday afternoon was pretty quiet."

I sighed. I hadn't expected her to know anything, but other than talking to Thelma, I didn't have any leads. Investigating a murder was way harder than it looked on TV. "Thanks. Text me if you hear anything."

"Sure thing." Julie nodded toward the center table before lowering her voice. "That's the person you want to talk to. She's been after Earl to marry her for years. Maybe she finally got tired of chasing, if you know what I mean."

I leaned forward. The idea of Thelma chasing Earl was news to me. The newspaper made it seem like they were just neighbors, but Kevin had said they were dating seriously. "What do you mean? Weren't they a couple?"

"Depends on what you mean. They've been sleeping together for ages, but Earl didn't want to commit. She tells everyone how serious they were, but most people know she was the only serious one."

Hmmm. If Earl didn't want to commit to Thelma, why the love statue? Was he interested in someone else? If so, maybe Thelma found out about it, and she's the one who attacked him in a fit of jealous rage.

All of a sudden, I felt less sure about going to question her. But at the same time, we were in a public place. She wasn't going to give a dramatic confession and then lunge at me like we were on her old show.

Partially to delay the inevitable and partially because he looked terrible, I paused to ask Rusty if everything was okay.

He sniffled. "Didn't you hear?"

"Yeah. I guess I didn't—"

"Earl was my favorite uncle."

My heart went out to him. "Oh, Rusty. I'm so sorry. I didn't know."

He wiped the back of one hand across his eyes and tried to cover it with a shrug. "I'm fine."

"Right. But if you ever need a friend, I'm just on the other side of that alley."

Poor guy. Now I wanted to know who killed Earl even more. Sure, I didn't know Rusty well, but he was a sweet guy. Plus, he'd given me the tip about Olive's job opening. If finding the answers could bring him some peace, I wanted to help.

With a fortifying sip of latte, I approached Thelma slowly, as if she were a wild bear. Except I would never approach a wild bear, because that's a terrible idea. Beside her sat a man I'd never seen before. Lean, with a sinewy kind of build, one gold earring, and gorgeous blue eyes. It was hard to tell because he was sitting, but the guy didn't appear to be much taller than Thelma. At least not taller than her hair. Unlike his companion, this man seemed to be fine with the aging process—he had gray hair, salt and pepper in his bushy eyebrows, and the lines in his face created a roadmap of the decades.

"Hi, Thelma. You don't know me, but I wanted to see how you're doing after what happened yesterday. It must have been really traumatic—"

"You! Oh yes, I know who you are." Despite the righteous indignation in her voice, not a single muscle in her face moved when she spoke. Creepy. "I know everyone in this town. And as you are well aware, that boss of yours killed my Earl!"

"Now, Thelma, hush. You can't go around accusing people." Her companion put one hand on her arm to calm her before turning to me. From the look in his eyes and my earlier conversation with Olive, I had a sneaking suspicion who he was before he spoke. "I'm Benji Turner."

"Nice to meet you," I said, trying to sound like I meant it. "I'm Aly. Aly Reynolds. My brother Kevin does estate planning and taxes and stuff."

"I know Kevin. What do you need?"

Thelma kicked Benji under the table. She must have thought it was subtle, but the sound of her heel bouncing off the metal table legs along with his yelp of surprise left little to the imagination. Benji shut up, fast.

Thelma spoke through gritted teeth. "We have nothing to say to you."

Me? What did I do? But before we got to that, I wanted to clarify this woman's relationship with Earl. "I'm sorry for your loss. Were the two of you close?"

"Close? We'd been courting for a couple of years now. I fully expected him to pop the question at any moment."

From the way she over-pronounced every single word, breathing heavily, I suspected the rumors of her acting in over a hundred love scenes weren't exaggerated. "I'm so sorry, Thelma. I didn't know."

"How could you? We like to keep things private in my generation, not like you young people posting everything on FaceGram or InstaBird."

I hid a snort of laughter behind my cup. That was rich, coming from the town gossip. But she was grieving, so I cut her some slack. "Can you tell me what happened?"

"You? Ha! You want to know what happened, go ask Olive! She's the one who had it out for my darling man." Her gaze moved away from me, darting around to see who was watching her performance.

This conversation wasn't going anywhere. Thelma was far more interested in keeping everyone's eyes on her than in having an exchange of information.

"Again, I'm sorry for what happened. But Olive didn't kill Earl." I started to tell her that I intended to find the real killer, but then I realized that, if Thelma *was* the real killer, I didn't want her to know I'd be investigating. "The police will figure it out."

"I am quite confident that they will. Mark my words, your boss is the guilty party." She sniffled and held the back of her hand to her forehead. "That is all I have to say today. Please go."

To punctuate her sentence, Thelma let out another theatrical wail and buried her face once more in the giant handkerchief. I didn't even know they came that big. It was practically a bedsheet.

Benji leaned forward, touched my arm. His hands felt like ice compared to the warmth of the shop. "The lady has asked you to go."

"Right. Sorry."

Everyone in the coffee shop was looking at us. When my eyes met Julie's, she tilted her head ever so slightly toward the exit. Obviously, I wasn't going to get anything useful out of Thelma, so I might as well leave before Benji escorted me out the door.

It was clear to see who ran Shady Grove. No one else would talk to me with Thelma glaring like that. I couldn't afford to antagonize the woman who not only was closest to the victim, but found his body. Especially when, at the moment, she was my number one suspect.

She had opportunity, being Earl's next-door neighbor and his possibly-serious-possibly-casual girlfriend. Either way, no one would find it odd to see her entering or leaving his house. If what Julie said was true, the fact that Thelma was more into the relationship than Earl could give her motive—especially if she found out that he was interested in someone else.

She looked like she was in decent shape. With the right weapon, she definitely had the strength to break someone's skull. I could do some tests to find out the amount of force required to apply that amount of pressure to the human head. That type of experimenting would keep Kyle entertained for hours. But if would help if I had any idea what the murder weapon was before I wasted an afternoon smashing fruit with random objects.

Things to worry about later. For now, it was time to go. If Thelma refused to talk to me, I'd have to find out how Earl died from someone else.

Unfortunately, I had no idea who.

9

The next morning, I headed for town immediately after dropping Kyle at preschool. It was a twenty-minute walk, and I didn't have to be at Missing Pieces until ten, but I hoped to talk to some other shop owners. With most people working or at school, Main Street shouldn't be busy.

It wasn't a big street. Other than Missing Pieces and Patti's Diner, we had a magic shop that never seemed to be open, a liquor store, clothing stores that catered to pregnant women and little kids, and the local bakery, plus a few other assorted businesses. Local regulations required name approval by the town council, which is why everyone had those cutesy names that made me roll my eyes in public. Secretly, I loved them. The town's personality might be my favorite thing about Shady Grove.

My feet came to a halt in front of a place I'd passed many times but never paid attention to. I Will Survive was a local self-defense studio, owned and operated by Olive's wife Maria. I hadn't met her yet, but we had a mutual interest in keeping my boss out of jail. She might have something useful to tell me. Like, did Olive happen to have blood all over her hands when she got home that night?

No. That was ridiculous. I refused to believe she might have been involved. She was at Missing Pieces when I left, and there was no reason to think she followed Earl home to murder him. If she'd been angry enough to kill him after their argument, she would have done it right there in the shop.

Helpful, Aly. Be sure to say that if you have to testify at Olive's trial.

From the sidewalk, the front of I Will Survive didn't look all that different from anyplace else on Main Street. Green wooden shutters placed over the windows were probably intended to provide privacy, but they matched the swinging wooden doors in a way that gave the place an old-time saloon vibe.

After a moment's consideration, I pushed the front door open and entered. The receptionist's area sat empty, but the door to the studio stood ajar. Since I didn't see anyone around, I moved closer. Two voices carried through the opening. Maria must be in the middle of a lesson. Since I couldn't come up with any good reason for interrupting, I used my phone to snap a picture of the contact info posted by the front desk. I'd text her or come back later.

Then I heard something that made me inch closer. A female voice said, "So you're not afraid anymore?"

Having never met Maria, I had no way of knowing if she was the person speaking. Was someone in trouble? Who were they afraid of? Was it Earl? Or maybe the person who killed him?

The responding voice trembled. "No. Everything is fine now."

"You understand why I'm unconvinced."

"I do. But it's over now. I overreacted." This time, the woman sounded more sure in her response. She seemed vaguely familiar, but I couldn't quite place her.

The woman who I was now pretty sure had to be Maria spoke again. "Okay. Well, I can't force you to keep taking lessons you don't want. Call me if you need anything. For now, I'll cancel your remaining sessions and give you a refund."

Footsteps echoed across the gym floor, coming nearer. I stepped away from the doorway, barely in time to avoid getting run into by Julie from On What Grounds?. With her red-rimmed eyes and puffy nose, she certainly didn't look fine. In fact, Julie might be the poster girl for "Not Fine."

Before I could ask what was wrong, she was gone, practically leaving skid marks on the carpet. I watched her go, replaying the conversation I'd overheard in my head.

Julie was afraid of someone. Afraid enough that she felt the need to take private self-defense lessons. But she didn't need to worry anymore? Maybe the danger had passed because the person threatening her was dead. Earl certainly had a temper. I could understand being afraid of him. That didn't make sense, though. If Julie killed him in self-defense, he wouldn't have a wound on the back of his head. And she'd said she was at work all day. Easy enough to verify.

Another woman appeared in the doorway. She was medium height, probably a couple of years older than Olive, with long wavy black hair, medium-brown skin, and huge brown eyes. Judging from the image on the poster hanging across from the front door, I deduced that this must be Maria.

See? I made an excellent detective.

A smile crossed the woman's face when she spotted me. "Aly? I had a feeling you'd be coming in."

A feeling? And how did she know my name? We'd never met. I glanced around and lowered my voice. "How do you know who I am? Do you have.... 'feelings' the same way Olive does? Special feelings?"

She laughed. "No. I wish. I recognized you from Olive's description. I'm Maria, obviously."

"Right. It's nice to meet you."

"You, too. I figured that, after everything that happened, you'd be dropping by. Call it women's intuition. Or, I don't know, maybe my wife is starting to rub off on me."

"Well, it would be great if you could rub off on her," I said. "She's not worried about being suspected of murder. Saying things to the police that make her look guilty."

"That's my girl. As honest as the day is long, always wants to believe the best in people. She won't even let me teach her a few moves to keep her safe. Says I can protect her if needed."

"That's sweet. Naive, but sweet."

"You're telling me." She shut her eyes for a moment before shaking her head. "How can I help you, Aly?"

Quickly I outlined the conversation between Olive and Officer Matthews, ending with a plea that she talk to her wife about hiring a lawyer, especially if Olive intended to speak to the police again. Kevin could refer her to someone. After she took a chance on me and gave me a job, I felt obligated to help. I also hated the idea of such a nice person getting blamed for something she didn't do.

Once Maria promised to talk to Olive, I asked her if she'd seen Earl after he left Missing Pieces. Of course she hadn't. I'd been the only person on Main Street when he zoomed off, because no one wandered around outside in January if they could avoid it.

"There's something that's been bugging me," I said.

"How did the killer get in and out without anyone seeing them? Thelma said she spent the entire day cooking, and if I know that woman, she's got her nose pressed to the window every second she's home."

"You're right about that," Maria said. "But surely she goes to the bathroom sometimes."

Especially when she drank tea for two hours every afternoon. Too bad we couldn't call and ask Thelma for her urination schedule. "Does she have a smart doorbell? That would show anyone who walked by. We might see something."

Maria snorted. "No. Thelma doesn't even have a cell phone. She's perpetually stuck in the early '90s, reliving her glory days on *As the Hospital Guides Our Lives*."

Well, that wasn't helpful at all.

"Does Earl's house have a back door?"

"Yeah. Those properties back up against the golf course. Big yards, largely shielded from flying balls by the trees that gave this town its name."

"So anyone could walk through the trees, cross Earl's backyard, and enter without being seen from the street?"

She nodded. "Yes, as long as Thelma's not in the kitchen. Her window faces Earl's backyard."

But Thelma had been in the kitchen, all day if she was telling the truth.

If.

10

A fter leaving I Will Survive, I turned left. At the end of the block, the wooden planks making up the sidewalk gave way to the more standard concrete. Second Street still displayed the wooden signs and quaint features of Main Street, but it lacked the cobblestones and raised sidewalks that gave Shady Grove that old time feel. Cutesy business names, however, remained. Thankfully.

Like most things in Shady Grove, We All Fall Down was about two blocks away. The white brick building sat at the back of a parking lot that would be considered tiny in most places, but was more than adequate by our standards. A giant wooden bowling ball and pins dominated the front of the building, with the name spelled out in red letters you could see from space.

Earl was an avid bowler, and competition for the number one spot in this town was fierce. How fierce, exactly? Was it worth killing for? To me, that sounded absurd, but so did wearing rented shoes.

When I entered the bowling alley, I stopped in my tracks

at the sight of the guy who was at On What Grounds? with Thelma behind the counter. What was he doing here? Hopefully he wouldn't scream at me until I ran out of the building the way she did.

At the moment, he leaned against the counter, chatting easily with a woman who sipped brown liquid from a large tumbler full of ice. She had short black hair cut in a bob, sharp brown eyes, and perfectly-shaped eyebrows. Let me tell you: eyebrows had to be pretty darn perfect for me to notice them.

Her pink and blue floral bowling shirt identified her as a member of the league, but not the same team as Kevin. Too bad. I'd like to see my brother in a shirt with giant pastel flowers. Maybe I could pay the woman who made them to "accidentally" slip the L back into his name when she stitched it on the front pocket.

I approached with what I hoped was a friendly smile. "Hi, I'm Aly."

Benji grunted. "I remember you."

The woman smiled. "Benji, be nice. I'm Wendy. Are you here to bowl?"

No. Not even a little bit. The last time I tried to bowl— heavy emphasis on *tried*—I somehow managed to bounce my ball across the lane into the one beside it, where it landed on this giant balloon that was there for some reason, promptly deflated it, and got stuck. When I went to retrieve my ball, someone screamed at me over the loudspeaker. The sound made me jump about three feet before falling over backward onto my butt. To make matters worse, I split my pants.

"Thank you, but no." Wendy, Wendy. That same sounded familiar. She lost the bowling tournament to Earl because of her dog. Probably not the best conversation starter. I grasped at the most convenient excuse I could think of to get them talking. "My brother wanted me to check and see if his bowling trophy came in. Kevin Reynolds."

Benji shook his head. "Sorry, not yet."

"No?" Wendy asked. "I thought they were due on Tuesday morning."

"Shipping delays. You know how it is. That postal service, messing everything up."

I took my opening. "Did you win a trophy, too?"

"Yeah. I took second place," she said. "Earl Parker won. Such a shame what happened to him."

Trying not to look excited that she'd taken the conversation exactly where I wanted, I shook my head sympathetically. "You knew him?"

Behind me, Benji barked out a laugh. "Did she know him? Hell, she's been chasing him for years!"

Whoa. Earl was starting to look like quite the ladies' man. Both Wendy and Thelma were after him? I dredged up a mental picture, but didn't see the appeal. Especially when, based on my limited experience, he did *not* have a great personality. I reminded myself that he was Rusty's favorite uncle and also dead.

"Gross. Don't make it sound like that." Wendy gagged, which relaxed me. "He's the top bowler in our league. I'm number two. But only because I missed the last game of the tournament. Poor Fluffykins will never know what she cost me. If I'd made it to the final game, I would have easily beaten him."

"Fluffykins?" She didn't know what Kevin had told me.

"Her pitbull," Benji said wryly.

"What happened to your dog?" I asked.

Wendy shook her head sadly. "I don't know. When I came home to change before the finals, she was in the backyard. She didn't come inside to greet me like usual, so I went to find her. Spotted the poor thing lying on the ground, eyes shut, next to a pool of vomit."

Aww. My heart went out to the dog. "That sounds terrible! Is she okay now?"

"Yeah, she's fine. The vet thought it must be something she ate. I don't know what, since I haven't changed her food in years, but maybe she caught a sick squirrel or something."

Or something. The people in Shady Grove were serious about bowling. Serious enough to poison a dog? And if so, would Wendy have killed Earl for doing it? "Could someone else have come into the yard and fed her something bad?"

Benji chuckled. "You've never met Fluffykins. That dog won't let anyone but Wendy within about forty feet."

"She'll attack?"

"She'll hide. Biggest 'fraidy dog I ever met."

"She's not afraid, she's discerning," Wendy said. "Just because she doesn't like you..."

This conversation was fascinating, yet completely off-track. "Is there any chance someone entered your yard to make Fluffykins sick on purpose?"

She shook her head. "No. The gates are double-locked because my neighbors have little kids. Fluffykins is the sweetest creature alive, but their younger girl is a terror. I can't risk her coming in when I'm not around to protect my sweet boy."

Hmmm. Kevin had said Wendy thought Earl poisoned her dog on purpose. Now she was saying Earl couldn't have gotten in to make the dog sick. It didn't make sense for my brother to make that up. Why would Wendy lie unless she was trying to cover up her motive?

My mind went to the fertility statue. "So you weren't interested in Earl? Do you know if he had feelings for you?"

She snorted. "Lord, no! He's been dating Thelma for years."

Yes, that's what everyone told me. It didn't explain why he wanted a love and fertility statue. They were too old to be seeking to conceive a child, so that didn't make sense. Maybe I had it all wrong. Maybe it was just the obvious, that he had the woman and needed the, er... functionality of the statue.

Gross.

Oshun was the goddess of many things. Earl could have gotten her to ask for rain to fill the rivers. Or anything other than fertility.

Benji eyed me. "You think Earl was cheating on Thelma?"

Wendy gagged again. "Not with me, he wasn't."

"To be honest, I don't know," I said. "I'm just wondering what happened to him. I always thought Shady Grove was a safe place to raise my nephew. But Thelma's telling the whole town Olive killed Earl."

"It wouldn't surprise me if Thelma killed him herself," Wendy said. "She's got one heck of a temper. If she saw another woman leaving his house, she might snap. There's the danger of dating your neighbor. Especially in a small town. No one has any secrets in Shady Grove."

No one except, apparently, the killer.

"If Earl were two-timing his neighbor, wouldn't he be smart enough to go to the other woman's house?" I asked. Both of them stared at me. "What?"

"Guessing you didn't know Earl," Benji said. "Smarts weren't exactly his strong suit."

My lips twitched. "I only met him once."

"Makes sense." Wendy nodded. "You wouldn't be asking."

Sigh. I wasn't getting anywhere. Time to be more direct. "Benji, you were here when Earl died, right?"

"Why? You get hired by police?"

My cheeks grew warm. I cast about for any reason I might be asking questions. "I'm a student. Doing research."

"Oh, yeah?" Wendy said. "Where do you go?"

"I'll be starting at Maloney College in a couple of weeks." Because molecular biologists spent a lot of time looking into murders. Remembering a show I'd streamed last fall, I said, "I want to be a true crime podcaster. One of my classes is on research and investigation. This seemed like a good opportunity to practice."

"So you want to fake interview me for a class you haven't started yet?" Benji asked.

"Yeah." It sounded dumb when he put it that way. Still not as dumb as me trying to use psychic powers to investigate a murder. "Is that okay?"

He shrugged. "Sure, I guess. Yeah, I was here on Wednesday night."

"Did anyone see you?"

"Other than all my customers?" He picked up a glass and started rubbing it. "We're open until ten every weeknight. At four-thirty, I've got a high school kid who runs the shoe rental counter and helps out in the arcade a couple nights a week."

Right. I'd seen a teenage girl behind the counter that time Kyle and I played here during Kevin's practice. I made a mental note to come back and talk to her before turning to Wendy. "What about you?"

Her face turned bright red. "On Wednesday? I was here, right, Benji? Bowling as usual. Just like Aly's brother."

He met her gaze levelly. "You came in late this week. I remember because you tracked salt from the parking lot all over the carpet."

"Oh, yeah. Sorry about that," she said. "I'd hoped the parking lot would be clear. I guess now it makes sense that it wasn't, with Earl dead and all."

"Maybe now you'll apologize for telling me my parking lot was a danger."

This conversation could go off the rails fast if I didn't intervene. I turned back to Wendy. "You were late? Why?"

"Fluffykins needed a little extra time outside, since I thought it might snow again. Anyway, my break's over. I need to practice." She pushed her now-empty glass across the counter to Benji and turned back toward the bowling lanes. "Thanks for the tea."

It didn't escape my notice that "I was with my dog" wasn't exactly an alibi. I couldn't call Fluffykins and ask if Wendy was telling the truth. Before I could prod further, she headed toward the lane. She definitely wasn't telling me something.

After a moment, she turned back. "Sounds like a fascinating class you're taking. Maybe I'll sign up."

"Are you a student?"

She grinned at me. "No, I work in the Maloney College admissions office. They give me a discount on classes."

The expression on her face left me praying that the school really did have a journalism department and a class on podcasting true crimes. Otherwise, she'd know I was lying before her next shift started. I'd put money on it.

But, I mean, if they didn't, they should. Those things were huge right now.

Benji took Wendy's dirty dishes and put them under the counter. "Anything else?"

"Do you think Earl was cheating on Thelma?"

"If he was, he wouldn't tell me. Thelma's my best friend." He shrugged. "We didn't talk much. He came in, he bowled, he left. Most people stuck with their own teams. Oh, except that girl who runs the coffee shop. Sometimes he'd hang around the counter, talking to her while waiting for his nachos."

"Julie?" Funny how her name kept coming up. She was tiny. She surely didn't have the strength to bash someone's head in. Except... without knowing what the murder weapon was, I couldn't possibly reach that conclusion. Also, some people were stronger than they looked. Simone Biles was tiny, too, and she was a powerhouse.

"Yeah."

The conversation I'd overheard at Maria's came back to me. "Did she look afraid at all?"

"Of Earl? Nah. Mostly, she looked like a pretty girl humoring some old creep who's wasting her time."

Having been that girl more than once in high school, I knew exactly what he meant. Still I added Julie to my mental list of suspects. She had been afraid of someone, she signed up for self-defense classes, and she didn't need them anymore. Even if Earl thought he was flirting with her (or using a love goddess on her?), that didn't mean Julie wouldn't feel threatened. And it didn't mean another man watching them from a distance would see her fear.

On the other hand—what if Earl really was innocently flirting with Julie...and Thelma noticed? On What Grounds? was the only place to get a good coffee in Shady Grove. The town's resident caffeine junkies were there at least twice a week, if not every day. It was completely reasonable to assume that he'd gone into the coffee shop at least once or twice. The possibility of Earl flirting with Julie in front of his girlfriend gave some support to my "jealous lover" theory. She could have been afraid of Thelma, not Earl. Or both of them.

Either way, with Earl dead, there wouldn't be any reason left to be afraid.

"Anyway, it was nice to see you again." Benji's voice broke into my thoughts. "I'll call your brother when the trophies come in."

"Right." I'd almost forgotten my excuse for dropping by in the first place. "Thanks."

A glance at the time on my phone told me that it was time to get to work. Olive wouldn't appreciate it if I arrived late for my second day on the job, even though I'd spent the entire morning trying to prove she wasn't a murderer. Really, she should pay me overtime. I'd already found two suspects who were more likely than my boss. Three, if you counted Thelma. Not bad for my first week of psychic detecting. (Especially considering I hadn't managed to use my powers intentionally yet.)

Lost in my thoughts, I tripped over the garbage can on my way back to the sidewalk. Awesome. It clattered to the ground, spilling a battered mess of wood and twisted metal onto my feet. Ouch. My knee and toes throbbed.

Given my murky control of my newfound powers, the last thing I wanted was to have a vision while picking up a stranger's garbage. Some things were personal. I still couldn't find my gloves, and I couldn't exactly use my coat to cover my hands while digging through trash. Apparently Benji had tossed the old trophies to make way for the new, and I didn't need to be bored by old bowling memories. Everything would have to stay where it was for now.

Sorry, Benji. I'd love to be able to pick up my mess, but it's not happening.

With a glance over my shoulder, I quickly walked away, hoping no one would call me back.

11

The jail/police station was located next to Town Hall, in the block between We All Fall Down and Missing Pieces, so that was my next stop. According to my brother, police reports were supposed to be public record in Shady Grove, but I sincerely doubted Doug would just hand it over. Still, I had to try. There could be something in the report that lead me to the murder weapon.

Finding the murder weapon could tell me exactly who killed Earl. All I had to do was get my hands on it, and I should get a vision of what happened. Probably. I hoped.

To my surprise, Julie exited the police station about half a block ahead of me. This time of morning, she should be at the coffee shop. She walked with purpose, glaring at the ground, tears streaming down her face. Before I could think about it, I stepped in front of her. "Julie? Are you okay?"

Her face went white at the sight of me. "What are you doing here?"

I thought fast. "I need to see Kevin before work."

She tilted her head at me. "I thought his office was closed on Fridays because he was in Albany."

Well, booger. She was right, but I hadn't expected her to know that.

I clapped one hand to my forehead in an exaggerated show of exasperation. "Is it Friday? I'm such a dummy. What a week! So... How are you?"

Too late, I realized I should've just told her I was dropping by to water his plants. No one would question that. Unless she'd been in his office and knew he didn't have plants.

Up close, the dark circles under her puffy eyes were apparent. Why was she walking out of the police station? Filing a report about the person who scared her? Or answering questions about the murder? I'd initially dismissed the idea because she was supposedly at the coffee shop, and she seemed so small. But she was a baker, and bakers grew strong from kneading dough. Add in her self-defense skills, and Julie could be a killer.

A good reason to get away from her, now that I thought about it.

Element thirty-three is arsenic. Element thirty-four is selenium...

"I'm fine," she lied. "Just tired."

It was on the tip of my tongue to ask why she'd been at the police station, but something told me not to give away my suspicions. First I needed to see if anyone could confirm her alibi. Instead, I smiled sympathetically. "Get some rest."

"You, too. Coffee will help." She paused, checking her phone. "Look at the time! Rusty will be waiting for me. Are you heading toward Missing Pieces?"

"Not yet." She waited for me to say more. Darn small towns where everyone talked about their business whether people wanted to hear it or not. "I need to go to Town Hall. About...a property line issue."

"With Mrs. Patel?"

Great. Of course she knew exactly who my neighbors were. This lying business was trickier than I thought. "No, the empty place on the other side. Long, very boring story. See you later!"

Since she apparently wasn't going to walk away first, I turned and bounded up the stairs to the Town Hall like that had been my destination all along. Oh, well. At least it was warm inside. I could defrost before heading next door to the police station. Maybe they had a side exit.

I wandered through the building, killing time until Julie was gone. Up one hallway, down another. The water department was housed here, apparently, and the tax authority. Fascinating stuff.

Finally, I found a hallway leading toward the police station. According to the sign on the wall, to my left would be the mayor's office, the ladies' room, and an exit. I started toward the last one.

As my footsteps clattered against the marble, voices carried to my ears. I skidded to a halt.

"Tim, this is big. I'm up for reelection this year. If you can't solve this, I could be facing a primary challenge this spring. We can't have a murderer on the loose."

The mayor. I recognized her voice from TV. Also, the sign on the wall told me her office was over here. Tim, Tim. Who was she talking to?

"I get it. But listen, I can't just go and arrest anyone without probable cause. We need to make it stick." The voice was unfamiliar, but since only police could arrest people, she must be talking to Sheriff Matthews. Doug had said his first name was Timothy.

The shadows on the floor told me they stood right

around the corner. If either of them moved a couple of feet in this direction, they'd see me.

I flattened myself against the wall, marveling about how good I'd gotten at listening to private conversations in just a few days. Once upon a time, I'd have walked by without even noticing that they were talking.

"Be sure it does. The first murderer in twenty years doesn't get away on my watch. *Especially* without even being arrested."

"I'm waiting for the coroner's report. It takes time. He's only in town one day a week."

A fist banged on the table. "We don't have time! We need to make an arrest today."

"Then get on the phone and tell him that." As Mayor Banister grew more agitated, Sheriff Matthews sounded increasingly calm. "Right now, I've got a man with a head wound and a missing cast iron skillet from his kitchen. That's not enough to charge anyone."

A missing skillet? I didn't know that. Made sense, though. Earl was found in his kitchen, and cast iron was heavy. Kyle asked me to buy him one for Christmas after seeing it on a cooking show. I had to get the four-inch one so he could lift it. Someone with enough strength to swing a large pan could cause real damage.

"What about the car? Thelma saw Olive's car outside Earl's house on Wednesday afternoon."

That gave me pause. My boss never mentioned leaving the store after me. I'd assumed she'd stayed until closing, which would have put her nowhere near the scene of the crime. Had she lied to me? And if so, did that mean what I thought?

Sheriff Matthews's voice cut into my thoughts. "We're looking into it. She never said it was Olive's car."

"Green Beetle? Come on." Mayor Banister scoffed. "How many of those are around here?"

"I understand you're upset, but we have to do this one by the book. I need to investigate all possibilities. Wait for DMV records, find the murder weapon, get the coroner's report. Interview Earl's friends and family. Question suspects. One thing at a time. Most murders aren't solved in a couple of days."

"Then why are you standing in my office?" She spat the words at him. "Get on it."

That was my cue to leave. I ducked into the ladies' room on the other side of the hallway right as footsteps moved toward the spot where I'd been hiding and listening. The door swung shut, and I leaned up against it until my heart stopped pounding.

Here's what I now knew:

1. Someone killed Earl by hitting him over the head with a heavy object.
2. A large cast iron skillet was missing from Earl's kitchen.
3. A car that might have been Olive's was parked outside at the time.
4. Olive and Earl argued right before he died.
5. Things weren't looking good for Olive.

Once Sheriff Matthews's footsteps receded, I left the restroom and headed back out into the cold. There was no longer any reason to go to the police station. The coroner's report wasn't finished yet. And the main reason I'd wanted the police report was to see what the murder weapon was. Now I knew.

A cast iron skillet would be easy to wield for someone

used to slinging around baking sheets and bowls and mixers. It would also be pretty simple to hide while looking for a way to permanently dispose of it, but I couldn't exactly go around town knocking on doors and asking to examine people's kitchens.

Where was the power to find lost objects when I needed it?

The time on my phone told me to stop skulking around and head to work for the day. At least, after what I heard, talking to Olive would naturally be the next step: why hadn't she told me that she'd gone to Earl's after he left the shop on Wednesday? What happened while she was there?

I shivered at the thought of her walking into a murder scene by mistake. But then why didn't she call the police? Was she hiding when Thelma showed up? If Olive had gotten there a few minutes earlier, she might have been in danger. My brain absolutely refused to consider the other potential implication of Sheriff Matthews's words. Olive didn't kill Earl. I couldn't explain how I knew, but I knew.

Once I made it inside the store, I stood against the back door for a long moment, soaking up the warmth. My body was numb, not just from the cold, but from everything I'd seen and overheard that morning. Element thirty-nine was yttrium. Y. Element forty was zirconium. Finally, I felt well enough to push away from the wood and hang up my coat, hat, and scarf.

A gust of wind blew the door open, sending an icy chill through the room. Just when I'd stopped feeling like a popsicle. I hurried to shut it before all the warm air leaked out.

The lock turned uselessly in its socket, spinning around without engaging. Weird. At least the knob clicked into place. That would have to be good enough for now.

"Hey, Olive," I said as I entered the main store. "Did you know the back door is broken?"

She looked up from her spot behind the counter, where she spoke into the store's cordless phone. "I'm so sorry. Are you coming up for the service?... Okay. Yeah...I understand... Listen, I've got to go... I love you, too."

She must be talking about Earl's funeral. With everything going on, it hadn't occurred to me that she might want to go. Of course she would. They had known each other a long time.

After she hung up, Olive turned to me. "Sorry, dear, that was Sam. He's really broken up about Earl's death."

"Really? They were friends?" Seemed like an odd pairing, but I was the first to admit I barely knew either of them.

"More than friends," she said. "Mowing lawns was Sam's first after-school job when he was twelve years old. He loved it. Later on, he was the one to convince Earl to incorporate, to expand the business. As much as I never liked Earl, he was a good male role model for my son."

Ah. Poor guy.

"That must be hard for him."

She nodded. "I wish I could do more. It's hard having him live so far away."

We could do more. We could find out who killed Earl, bring Sam some closure, and take suspicion off his mother. Based on the conversation I overheard at Town Hall, police weren't even looking at anyone else. Which reminded me—I needed to ask Olive about her visit to Earl's house on Wednesday afternoon.

Before I could open my mouth, the bells above the front door jingled. For the second time in two days, a police officer stepped slowly and deliberately across the threshold, into the store. This time it wasn't Doug, the young and relatively easygoing deputy. Sheriff Matthews stepped onto the Welcome mat, along with an officer I'd never seen before. I shivered at the rush of cold air swirling through the room.

"Welcome to Missing Pieces," Olive said. "Good morning."

"Thank you. Sorry we can't say the same," Sheriff Matthews said.

"You can't say good morning?" Olive asked. "What's going on?"

Sheriff Matthews held up a sheet of paper. "We've got a warrant to search the premises."

"What? How?" I said.

He barely glanced at me. "You and your employee will wait outside until we're done. My nephew is by the car, and he can answer any questions."

Olive took the paper and scanned it once, twice. "You want to look for the murder weapon? Here?"

Oh, dear. Our supply of housewares took up a quarter of the far wall. Plenty of those things could be used to murder someone, just like in any kitchen shop. Pots, pans, vases, skillets...and Earl was hit over the head with a skillet. A chill went down my spine that had nothing to do with the cold air blowing through the still-open door.

I didn't for a second believe that whatever killed Earl would be found inside Missing Pieces. But I heard Mayor Banister in the back of my head, urging the sheriff to arrest someone, anyone. Olive was already a suspect, and now they were guaranteed to find something in the shop that could easily double as a murder weapon. Her fingerprints would be on everything.

Sheriff Matthews wasn't likely to listen to me, so I went straight outside to Doug while the other officer pulled on rubber gloves and began to search. "What's going on? There's no evidence Olive had anything to do with this."

"Uncle Tim's got a warrant that says otherwise."

"I don't understand." Items clanged inside, and I cringed. They were destroying Olive's livelihood in there, all because the Mayor wanted another term.

He studied me for a long moment, and then he sighed. "I shouldn't be telling you this, but we got an anonymous tip."

"A tip?"

"Someone said that if we looked inside the store, we'd find the murder weapon."

"Of course you would! Doug, we have an entire wall of household goods. We also sell antique crossbows in there. Knives, guns. Half the items in the store could be used to kill someone, if you tried hard enough."

A surge of voices went up inside the store. I couldn't make out what they were saying, but a moment later, Sheriff Matthews appeared in the doorway, holding a large cast iron skillet in his gloved hands.

"This is stupid," I said. "All cast iron skillets look the same. We've got the same one at my brother's house." Just about one-fifth of the size.

"Oh, you do?" Sheriff Matthews turned the skillet in his hands. "And is yours engraved with 'Earl and Nicole, May 4, 1984'?"

Olive gasped.

My mouth fell open. I couldn't speak. There had to be a reasonable explanation. Earl must've donated the pan. Or Nicole. Who was Nicole?

Time slowed. Sheriff Matthews stepped down out of the doorway and moved toward us. I wanted to run, wanted to hide. Wanted to do anything other than continue to witness this moment.

When he reached Doug, Sheriff Matthews handed him the skillet. I hadn't noticed earlier that he also wore gloves. "Bag this, please."

"Yes, sir."

Then he turned to the two of us. "Olive Green, you're under arrest for the murder of Earl Parker."

12

No. This couldn't be happening.

My mind reeled as Sheriff Matthews recited the litany of rights I'd heard on a million cop shows. Someone must've set this up. It was too big a coincidence. First, the mayor insists that the police arrest someone, and then they find the murder weapon in our store? Based on an anonymous tip. I didn't buy it. Of all the reasons to believe Olive didn't kill Earl, she wasn't stupid enough to try to sell the murder weapon. Not when she could've just wiped off the handle and left it on Earl's stove.

Beside me, my boss must've been in as much shock as I was, because she hadn't moved or blinked since Sheriff Matthews's proclamation.

"Olive, I'm going to need you to come with me," he said.

"We've known each other for forty years, Tim. I can't have heard you right."

"Let's not make this a bigger scene than it has to be. I'm going to cuff you and put you in the back of my car. Then we're going to drive to the police station."

"No cuffs. Please." I made my plea to Doug, who'd

finished whatever he needed to do with the skillet. "She'll get in the car willingly, won't you?"

She nodded, her face white.

Sheriff Matthews studied her. Other shop doors opened, and people started to filter out onto the sidewalk. Somehow, someone must've figured out what was going on. The whole town would be here soon at this rate. Poor Olive needed to go if she didn't want everyone to witness her humiliation.

"Don't say a word to anyone," I said as Doug moved Olive toward the car. "I'll call Kevin."

She turned her head toward me. "Call Maria for me? Please."

"I will," I promised. "Don't worry, Olive. We'll get you out of there ASAP."

By the time I got off the phone with my brother, the store was hopping. People had clearly heard what happened and were coming in to see if Olive was behind the register as usual or if the rumors were true. I both hated and understood them.

Until last week, the biggest news since I'd moved to Shady Grove was the debate over who owned the Changs' cat. That was a rough divorce. It made the front page of the *Shady Grove Globe*, which said more about the lack of news in our town than the level of interest people had in the case. Still, rubbernecking sure felt better on the other side.

There was no way I could call Maria now, with people all over the store waiting to overhear any bit of gossip. Instead I texted Kevin, asking him to contact Olive's wife for me. He replied immediately, which at least gave me one less thing to worry about.

Poor Olive. She must be freaking out.

Meanwhile, I berated myself for not finding that stupid skillet myself. If I'd known the murder weapon was *in the store*, I could have put my hands on it already and solved this whole thing. Theoretically.

Sheriff Matthews only arrested my boss because Mayor Banister was putting pressure on him. I knew it. But how did the pan get into our kitchenware section? Most of our stock came from estate sales and inheritances, but people did come in and sell things once in a while. Surely Olive would have mentioned if she'd bought a pan belonging to Earl from someone else in the past two days.

By the time the store cleared out, I was completely exhausted. The only thing I wanted was to close the doors and go home and go to bed. I wouldn't, of course. I'd made a commitment, and I needed to stay here until the regular closing time. But I did sit down and check my phone to see if there was any word from Kevin. Three new texts awaited.

Kevin: My friend Jake is on his way to see Olive now. He's a defense lawyer in Willow Falls. Should be there soon.

Kevin: Mrs. Patel got Kyle from preschool, no problem. She can watch him until four.

Unknown: Aly, it's Sam. I got your number from Mama. Driving up now. Call me when you get a chance?

Under ordinary circumstances, that third message would have been ignored. I didn't call people. In fact, my outgoing voice mail message said, "I don't check this. Text me." But Sam was on the road, and I preferred to talk to him before he finished the three-hour trip from New York City to Shady Grove, so I made an exception.

"Hey," I said as soon as he answered. "How is she?"

"I don't know. I haven't talked to her yet."

"I thought she gave you my number."

"No. Mama gave me your number. *Mom* is the one in jail."

"Oh, okay. Sorry. What's up?"

"First, thank you for being there to take over the store today."

"No problem. It's literally my job," I said. "I just didn't anticipate being left in charge during my first week. My brother Kevin sent a lawyer to talk to your mom. He's probably already there."

"Thank you so much," he said. "Do you know what happened?"

I relayed the morning's events, including most of the conversation at Town Hall. "Hey, that reminds me. I didn't get a chance to ask Olive earlier. Does your mom own a green Beetle?"

"Sort of. That's my car," he said. "My moms gave it to me as a graduation present last year. Why?"

"Because Mayor Banister said a green Beetle was parked in front of Earl's house on Wednesday and that places Olive at the scene of the crime."

He let out a heavy sigh, so loud I practically felt the rush of air through the phone. "Oh, man. This is all my fault."

"What are you talking about?"

"It's my car. I was at Earl's."

Hang up, Aly! The little voice inside my head screamed. I ignored it. Sam was in the car on the highway, nowhere near Shady Grove. He couldn't hurt me.

Also, according to the internet, he'd been long gone by the time Earl wandered into Missing Pieces. Sam couldn't be the killer unless he also possessed the ability to teleport or he'd convinced a museum to post fake pictures of him all over their social media.

"What time were you there? And why?"

"I went right after I left Missing Pieces, so about twenty minutes before noon."

Long before Earl died. So long, it didn't even make sense

to mention the car at all. Someone really wanted Olive to look guilty.

Sam continued, "I've done the books for Earl's gardening and snowplow company since high school."

"I thought you were just learning to be an accountant."

"I'm just getting the MBA now, but I've been working with numbers for ages," he said. "And I've got an accounting degree."

"Your mom told me you and Earl were close," I said. "I'm sorry for your loss."

"Yeah, thanks." His voice thickened. "Listen, I've got to go. But I want you to know, I appreciate everything you're doing for us. Most people in your shoes would have run away by now."

Most people didn't need their new boss to help them with the psychic powers they never knew they had. With everything going on, I'd barely had a chance to even think about what to ask her.

"Your mom's a special lady," I said instead. "I want to help."

"Thanks. I'll drop by after I talk to my moms. Meanwhile, take a break. Go get some coffee. The store will be fine for a few minutes."

I started to object, since I didn't have a key to lock up the store while I was gone. Then I remembered that the back door was broken. I hadn't gotten a chance to mention it to Olive. Instead, I told Sam.

"That's odd. It worked fine on Wednesday."

Wednesday morning seemed like a hundred years ago. I couldn't believe it had only been two days. "Are you sure?"

"Positive. I hauled a bunch of trash out that way after building Mom's bookcase. Then I locked it behind me, because that's the best way to keep it from blowing open in the wind. The latch doesn't always take."

Huh. If the lock had worked on Wednesday, but it was broken now, someone must've come into the shop in the past forty-eight hours. That explained how Earl's skillet got into the store. It gave credence to my "Olive's been framed" theory. Now I just needed to figure out who was framing her and why. Would Sheriff Matthews have planted evidence and made up a fake tip to appease the mayor?

No. There was no time. Unless he'd brought the pan in before I overheard them. But maybe that's what Julie was doing at the police station when I saw her—leaving a "tip."

"Okay, thanks. I'll talk to you later," I said. "And Sam?"

"Yeah?"

"Call a locksmith before someone else plants murder evidence in the store." I hung up before he could reply.

On What Grounds? was even busier than Missing Pieces had been, if that was possible. More people gathered in that tiny space than I realized lived in the town. Steel bands wrapped around my chest, making it impossible to draw breath.

Element seventy-eight is platinum. Pt. Element seventy-nine is gold. Au, for some reason. G was available.

This wasn't working. The weight of the gaze of a dozen people standing in line crushed me. Coming here was supposed to give me a break, help me relax, but it had the opposite effect. Did I really need coffee that badly?

Nope. Not worth it. Lattes were overrated. Olive had a coffee maker in the back room. I could leave the store closed for half an hour, make my own pot, and gather my thoughts.

Just as I turned to go, a voice called my name. Rusty. The whispers stopped. To my dismay, the crowd parted, leaving me a clear path to the register.

"Hey! Sorry, I only have a few minutes. I'll come back later."

"Don't be ridiculous! We know you're busy. Here, come to the front of the line," he said.

This must be what it felt like to be a superstar. Or, you know, the closest non-relative to a person recently arrested for committing the first murder in Shady Grove in several decades. I didn't delude myself for a second that my long-ago movie nights with Rusty resulted in this type of service.

Today he was working the register while Julie made the drinks. Too bad, because I had a lot of questions for her at the moment. I'd need to come up with some other way of finding out what was going on with her. Like...asking her store manager. Who I sort of had an in with, if you counted those two really awkward dates where we had nothing to talk about.

Okay, maybe not.

He saw me looking and whispered out of the corner of his mouth. "Are you okay?"

I shook my head, almost imperceptibly, then raised my voice as I put a crumpled five-dollar bill on the counter. Using my debit card took longer. "I'll have a low-fat vanilla latte with extra foam, please. To go."

"No problem." He reached out and put his hand over mine. "It's on the house."

The unexpected gesture made me look up to meet his gaze. The compassion in his eyes brought tears to mine. I blinked rapidly, refusing to shed them. "Thank you."

"Why don't you go back to the store?" he said. "I'll bring it over in a few minutes."

"Oh, I couldn't. You've got a ton of people waiting."

"It's fine. Olive's a friend." He took a deep breath. "The Mayor's doing a press conference outside Town Hall in a few minutes. Everyone's going to be streaming it, so you probably don't want to be here."

"I don't suppose you could accidentally shut off the Wi-Fi?"

"Probably not without Julie noticing. Anyway, I don't want you to have to deal with watching Thelma's reaction." He tilted his head to his left, and for the first time, I noticed the woman holding court at a table surrounded by onlookers. In fact, every head in the room that wasn't pointed at me watched her. Thelma glared at me with distaste evident on her face.

This was getting ridiculous. Time to take charge.

Clearing my throat, I walked toward her. "I'm sorry, but can I help you?"

She gasped. "How dare you speak to me?"

"Well, you're staring at me like I kicked your puppy, so it seemed like you'd have something to say."

She continued to open and close her mouth, looking more like a fish needing air than a famous actress. "Well, I never!"

"You never what? Had anything nice to say about anyone? This is ridiculous. I didn't kill Earl. I'm just trying to get coffee. You sit here on your little throne, presiding over all the gossip in Shady Grove because you want to feel important. If you want to be important, try doing something useful for a change."

The room was so silent, you could've heard a pin drop. Every eye in the place was glued to me and Thelma. She looked thunderstruck, and so did several patrons. Apparently no one ever stood up to her.

When she didn't answer, I shrugged. "I've got to get back to work. Nice to see you again."

"You tell your boss that she'll pay for what she did to my

Earl!" The words burst out of the woman like gunfire. She held one hand to her mouth as if she wanted to take them back.

"Olive didn't do it. But I hope they find the person who did."

Since Rusty had already agreed to bring my coffee over when it was ready, I didn't wait around to hear her response. My heart pounded as I exited the cafe, my overactive imagination envisioning a swarm of people following and sweeping me down the street to avenge Earl's death. Of course, that was silly.

Lost in thought, I slipped. My left foot went out from under me. Reaching out, I struggled to keep my balance, but the alley wasn't nearly as well-salted as the main roads. No one used the path between the store and the coffee shop except, well, me. I went down on one knee, hard. Ow. My hands plunged into the snow patch lining the edge of the building.

What on earth...?

Grumbling to myself, I got to my feet and wiped the snow and salt off my pant leg. I never should have left California. Not once did I trip over all the glorious sunshine.

After a moment, I spotted the item that caused my fall. It wasn't ice, like I thought. It was like a linen bath towel, which made no sense. Then I spotted the stains and the big monogram in the center. Ew. Not a bath towel. I was holding a used, snotty handkerchief. What was it doing here?

I didn't know, and I didn't particularly want to find out. It could just stay there. Well, off to the side, anyway. I flung the thing away so no one else would slip on it.

Back inside the store, I scrubbed my hands vigorously while chanting the introduction to *Star Trek* twice. It only took twenty seconds to say once, but I liked to be extra thorough. Then I unlocked the front door, flipped the sign to OPEN, turned the phone forwarding off, and braced myself for whatever came next. The answer, it turned out, was not much. Everyone was probably going to watch the Mayor's fake press conference, where she patted herself on the back for arresting the wrong person.

A smattering of flashbulbs outside the windows sent me to the front of the store. Too late, I spotted the podium in the middle of Main Street and the growing audience that told me Mayor Banister's press conference had apparently moved from Town Hall. What was wrong with that woman? She had some nerve! It took all my restraint to keep from marching out there and giving her a piece of my mind.

I spent five minutes pacing around and dusting every-thing before the bell over the front door jingled. Nothing I touched gave me any feelings at all, which was exactly how I liked it. It was all just stuff with dust on it that looked some-what cleaner after I finished. Olive kept the place practically gleaming to start, so my efforts didn't make much difference.

"Aly? Are you here?"

Rusty. I'd almost forgotten that he was bringing me coffee. He stood in the doorway holding a tray covered by a battered old silver dome. Seriously old. Like, I was pretty sure he'd bought it in this store. He set the tray on the front counter and lifted the lid, revealing two massive teacups and two plates each holding a chocolate croissant.

"Oh, man. This was so unnecessary, but I could kiss you right now."

His face turned bright red, and I thought back to those not-remotely-thrilling dates.

"I'm sorry—I didn't mean..." Great. Now he probably thought I'd spent all this time pining for him. "Thank you."

"You looked like you could use a friend."

I gestured toward the small table where Olive originally interviewed me. "Do you want to sit? I know you've got a lot of customers to get back to."

"Not anymore. Just about everyone is outside, listening to the Mayor." The sound I muttered under my breath was halfway between a growl and a curse word. Rusty ignored it and said, "Anyway, Julie's got things covered."

Right. The owner could take care of her own store for a bit. Excellent! Getting Rusty alone gave me an opportunity to ask about his boss's relationship with Earl.

Lifting my mug, I inhaled the steam, drawing fortification from the mingling odors of milk and espresso. Rusty even dusted the top of the drink with cinnamon, a touch that once again left me marveling at his consideration. My body's response was purely Pavlovian when I relaxed against the chair.

I took a big gulp, savoring the taste. Then I choked.

13

For the third time in less than forty-eight hours, the room fell away.

I sat in a high-backed chair like on old British TV shows, in parlors or whatever. Faded pink flowers decorated a cream background. In a matching chair to my left sat an old man I'd never seen before, with a long scar down the side of his face. He reached one hand out, and I took it. Not my hand, though. The fingers reaching out to grasp his were wrinkled, knotted. The hand of an old lady.

Our eyes met. He mouthed, "I love you."

I started to say, "I love you, too," but the words never came.

Everything went black.

The cup slammed back onto the table, spilling coffee everywhere. "What happened? What did you do?"

He tilted his head at me. "I just made a pot of lattes. Is something wrong?"

Yeah. I'll say. Oh, man. Of all the times to get another vision. But I couldn't tell Rusty what I saw. The whole town already looked at me funny because of Olive. So I lied. "I'm sorry. It's just...hotter than I expected."

C is for carbon. Ca is for calcium. Cl is for chlorine.

I fanned my face several times while he studied me, probably thanking his lucky stars that we'd never gone on a third date.

"Right. Too hot." He paused as if waiting for me to say something. Then he let out a sigh and ran his hands over his hair. "Look, I should be going. Bring the tray back whenever. Or Julie can come and get it."

"Thank you. Sorry. I'm just overwhelmed by everything that's happened. It's my first week on the job."

"Of course. I'll talk to you later."

I watched him go, wondering why I couldn't seem to control these things. Then a thought hit me as he reached the front door. I called out to him.

Rusty half turned. "Yeah?"

"This tea set. Does it belong to the coffee shop?"

He gave me a quizzical look. "No, it's Julie's, but she keeps it in the back for special occasions. I found it for her at an estate sale a few years ago. An elderly couple got it as a wedding gift, at least according to the executor. Married sixty years, then they died sitting side-by-side, holding hands."

Exactly the scene from my vision. Whoa. This was bananas. I cleared my throat. "I, uh, like the pattern. Thought I might get something similar."

"Yeah. It's nice. Is that it?" He eyed me suspiciously. "Or did you have a vision when you drank your latte?"

This time, I choked for real. I hacked and coughed until tears came to my eyes. Rusty came over and patted my back helpfully.

"Thanks."

"Nice evasion tactics."

Well, a girl had to try. I smiled sheepishly. "How did you

know? Do you have powers? Or visions? Or whatever this is."

He shook his head. "Man, I wish. I didn't know, I guessed. Olive opened this place when I was a little kid, and you're the first person she's ever let work here besides Sam."

Interesting that he would be so direct about my boss's powers. For some reason, I thought they were secret. "Wait. Do people know about Olive? Can she really do what she says?"

"I don't know what she says she can do. But there's something about her. A couple of years ago, when I'd first started working at the coffee shop, I found a bag under a table after closing. Full of cash, no ID. I was trying to figure out what to do with it when Olive came in."

Although I could sense where this story was going, I played dumb. "It was hers?"

"Nope. I thought she was going to claim it. She saw the money. But instead, she put one hand on the fabric, closed her eyes, and told me Principal Spaulding left it there."

"From the preschool?" I summoned up a mental image of the man who presided over drop off and pick-up every morning. Perfectly rigid spine, perfectly combed comb-over. He didn't seem the sort to carry a bag full of money *or* to lose it.

"Yeah. She tried to play it off like she'd seen him with it, but her story didn't add up. Anyway, I called him. Asked if he'd left anything behind in the store. He described the bag perfectly, told me all about how the school had done a big fundraiser, raised a lot of money—and he'd lost it."

"The bag you found."

"Right. He came in, I gave it back. He tried to give me twenty bucks for my honesty."

"Did you tell him about Olive?"

He shook his head. "Nah. Partially because it's not my thing to tell. But also because I didn't know how to explain. It sounded nuts."

"Yeah. What a weird coincidence, huh?"

"Yeah. Do you know what the most interesting part of the story is?"

I shook my head. "The reward?"

You don't seem at all surprised by what I just told you."

D'oh. This past week was really putting my acting skills to the test, but I kept failing.

"Um, well, I've seen some weird stuff lately." Like he said, Olive's secrets weren't mine to share. Not even with someone who already strongly suspected.

If I managed to find the murder weapon and she saw the owner, that would be soon enough for us to share her powers with the rest of the town. Unless the killer had used something already in Earl's house. Like his own skillet.

Argh!

"Is that why you're helping me?" I asked. "You think I'm like her?"

"Not the only reason. Olive's good people. She doesn't deserve to be blamed for something she didn't do." His face fell. "So you can't do what she does?"

I couldn't, but that was irrelevant. We didn't need to know who *owned* the murder weapon. We needed to know what it was, who used it, and why. My abilities might be more useful than hers, if only I could figure them out.

After another moment's hesitation, I decided to trust Rusty. For one thing, I could use a friend. But he also seemed to accept the stuff I had trouble believing. Maybe he could help.

"No." I took a deep breath. "Honestly, I'm not sure what I can do. But there's something."

"That's too bad. I was hoping you could help me find out what happened to Uncle Earl."

"I really want to," I said. "I'm just not sure how."

He smiled shyly. "Maybe we can figure it out together."

If I didn't know better, I might have thought he was flirting with me. But considering his vast disinterest after our date and recent loss, I didn't let myself get too excited by that notion. "Tell me about your uncle."

Rusty shrugged. "Not much to tell. What you saw was what you got with Uncle Earl. I'm sorry you met him under such awkward circumstances. Generally, he was a fun guy. People loved him."

Reaching over, I squeezed his hand. "I'm sorry for your loss."

"Thanks."

"Do you have any idea who might have done this? Did you see Earl on Tuesday?"

"Sorry, no. I was at the coffee shop from noon to closing. Julie was teaching me some of her recipes."

With Julie. All afternoon. Earl died after he came into Missing Pieces, so during Rusty's shift. If Julie was working with him, she couldn't have killed Earl.

"You were both there from lunch to closing?"

"Yup. Every Tuesday."

Great. There went my only suspect. Although I liked Julie and was glad she wasn't a killer, that didn't help me figure out who did it.

People on TV made this look so easy. There had to be a way to figure out what happened.

"Did he have any other family?"

"My parents. They moved to Florida a few years back. I have an aunt in Chicago, but I was his only family in town. My grandparents died years ago."

The name from the back of the cast iron skillet came back to me. "Who was Nicole?"

Rusty's eyes widened. "Aunt Nicole? We don't talk about her. Apparently she and Earl were married before I was born, but she moved away when they divorced. I never met her."

Well, that explained the date.

"Did they have any kids?"

"No."

"What about close friends? Earl and Thelma were dating, right?"

"Yeah. For a couple of years now. I think she was more into him than he was, to be honest. Not to speak ill of the dead, but it seemed like he was only with her because she lived next door and he was too lazy to go meet someone else."

Ouch. Poor Thelma. I mean, she was horrible, but that was harsh. "Did she know?"

"I doubt it. She thought they were in love."

Not the first time I'd heard that, but I'd thought Thelma was exaggerating their relationship for the sympathy. Now it sounded like her designs on happily ever after were real, if not reciprocated.

"Did he plan to marry her?" I asked. "She seemed to think they'd be getting engaged soon."

"No. No way."

"You're sure?"

"Yeah, positive," Rusty said. "He'd been talking about breaking things off because she was too clingy. No way he was about to propose. I don't care what Thelma said."

A thought struck me. "Just how badly did she want to marry Earl?"

His eyes widened. "Do you think she killed him because he turned her down?"

"I don't know. Maybe. All I know is, someone had a motive. Someone killed Earl, and it wasn't Olive." I shook my head and sighed. "Let's get to work."

Quickly, I filled him in on what happened when I tried on the ring, my subsequent conversation with Olive, my efforts to find a reasonable explanation, my attempts to "read" Earl's statuette, the textbook, and the vision I'd just had. By the time I finished, he had such a mixed look of awe and wonder on his face, I expected him to either run away or kiss me.

"This never happened before you visited Olive's shop? You had no idea you could do this?"

"Nothing I can think of." I shrugged. "My parents were really into modern stuff. We didn't have any antique furniture. As far as I remember, we never visited second-hand shops. No yard sales, no used clothing stores, not even Goodwill. Not...once."

Now that I heard the words, that sounded very odd indeed. Who went their whole life without visiting a garage sale? Especially growing up in the suburbs, where we drove by them practically every weekend in the summer. Dad always said we had enough stuff, that we didn't need more. But suddenly, I wondered if there was more to it.

"You didn't have anything in your house that belonged to someone else? Nothing passed on from a grandparent or a great-aunt?"

I thought for a minute. "Not to my knowledge. My aunts and uncles are all alive. My grandmother died when I was a kid. Mom put her stuff in storage right away. She said—."

Realization hit me like a ton of bricks.

"Let me guess. She didn't want you to touch any of it."

"She said I wasn't ready for the pain that would come with being around things owned by someone I loved so much. I always thought she was talking about grief."

"She could have been," he said. "It would've been painful to relieve your grandmother's memories."

For the first time, I wondered if Mom shared my powers. If not, how did she know? Was I hit by lightning as a baby? Olive had said that powers sometimes manifested when a person turned twenty-one, but maybe it was genetic. Did Kevin know anything?

Maybe it was some mixture of getting saddled with a weird name and turning twenty-one, and my brother escaped only because he'd had the good sense to get a name change.

Or, you know, maybe I'd been watching too many conspiracy movies.

With a moan, I sank back into my chair and buried my head in my hands. "None of this makes any sense."

"We'll figure it out."

"Hoooooooooooooooooow?" It was more a moan than a word.

A long silence followed my proclamation. I'd have thought Rusty abandoned me, except the bell over the door didn't ring. There was no sneaking in or out of Missing Pieces. Finally, he snapped his fingers, and I raised my head.

"Okay, I've got it! You like science right?" The fact that he remembered this random fact from our date brought a small smile to my face. It wasn't a major topic of conversation.

"Yeah. I'm getting a degree in molecular biology."

"Excellent. Let's do some experiments."

Right. That made perfect sense, but things had been so

weird this week, it hadn't occurred to me. "To test the limits of my powers?"

"Exactly." He gestured around us. "You're in an antique shop. Everything here has belonged to someone else at one point. So let's touch some stuff and see what happens. I'll help."

"You want me to walk around the store while the owner's not here and play with all the items we're trying to sell? For science."

"For science!"

When he put it like that, how could I refuse? Especially with that impish glint in his eyes. This could be fun. "Okay? Where do we start?"

After some thought, I wandered over to the clothing section. Olive had a huge selection of antique clothes, but I hadn't spent much time there. There was nothing from my lifetime, and I tended to wear casual, comfortable clothes. I didn't have a lot of use for a flapper dress. But as I looked, I made a mental note to do my Halloween shopping here from now on. We had some nice stuff in our stock, and I probably got a discount.

I should find out about that, actually.

With a deep breath, I reached out and touched the item nearest me, a pinstripe men's suit that looked like a costume from *Chicago*. Nothing happened. I tried one dress, then a high-necked blouse. My hand skimmed the racks, touching everything. Nada.

Frustrated, I stomped my foot. "This isn't helping Olive!"

"Hold on," Rusty said. "Your first vision was when you wore the ring, right?"

"Yeah."

"You didn't feel anything from just picking it up?"

"No, but I put it on pretty much right away."

"True. Okay, but then you held the statuette of Oshun and felt nothing, right? You thought your powers were gone."

"Right. I didn't have another vision." A squeal escaped me. I hugged Rusty with all my might. "You're a genius!"

"Heh. I haven't said anything yet."

"You think I need to *use* an object to get a vision from it."

He nodded. "It's only a hypothesis, but yeah."

"Right." It occurred to me that I still clutched his sides. Clearing my throat, I stepped back. Way back. "Sorry. Okay, let's perform an experiment. I need to try the clothes on."

"Here. This looks about your size."

I turned to look at where Rusty pointed and immediately, my hands went to my mouth. A gorgeous wedding dress that had to be from the 1920s, with an empire waist and folds of lace that fell elegantly to the ground. "Oh, I couldn't. I don't want to see some poor woman who died at her wedding."

"You could have a happy vision, you know. Most people have pleasant memories of their wedding day."

True, but so far I'd only seen people die. Well, I didn't know what happened to the textbook owner, but it had looked like a scary amount of drugs. Doubtfully, I said, "I hope you're right."

"Come on, whoever wore this dress probably died seventy years later. Most items in these places come from estates."

"You know, that doesn't make me feel any better." But now that the dress had caught my attention, I couldn't tear my eyes away. For some reason, I wanted to wear it. Wanted to see how I looked with the snug bodice and capped sleeves. I tried one last argument. "It's got about four thousand buttons up the back."

"I'll help you. Come on. Let's try it."

Grabbing the dress, I went into the fitting area to try it on. Really, it would fit over my leggings just fine, but if I were going to do this, might as well get the full effect. The "room" was basically two square feet with a chair in one corner, sectioned off from the rest of the store by an old curtain.

I stepped out of my boots, whipped my sweater off, and shimmied my pants down my legs. A shiver went down my spine. Whether from the cool air in the room or the importance of what we were attempting to do, I didn't know.

A moment later, the silk whispered over my head, falling to the floor. The full-length (also antique, fifty percent off) mirror was in the main area, so I couldn't see how I looked, but it fit my upper body like a second skin. A glance down revealed cleavage I'd never known I could possess. I should see if Olive sold other corset tops if this was the effect. But other than a sense of wonder, I felt nothing.

Peeking around the dressing room curtain, I motioned for Rusty to come button me up. Then I spun around while he closed the back of the gown for me. His hot breath touched my neck, his strong hands comforting against my back. This was the closest I'd stood to a non-relative in over a year.

It was on the tip of my tongue to ask what happened, why he never called me after our second date. But now wasn't the time. First I needed to find out who killed Earl and get Olive out of jail, then I could worry about my love life.

Correction: *first* I needed to have a vision.

Rusty slid the final button through the hole, locking the gown into place. I shook out the folds of the skirt, then twirled around.

A strange man knelt in front of me, holding out a ring. A simple gold band. A sense of love and wonder came over me. As I watched, the ring slid onto my finger. A voice said, "I now pronounce you man and wife!". The man leaned in for a kiss. Then everything blurred together.

When I came back to my senses, Rusty cradled me in his arms. We still stood in the doorway of the dressing room. "Whoa there. Are you okay?"

I sniffled and wiped my eyes. "I saw something, but it wasn't the owner's death. It was her wedding day. Her husband had such love on his face. It was beautiful."

"Who was he?"

A very lucky man? No one ever put that expression on my face. I shrugged the thought away. "No idea. He's probably not even still alive. But now we have data!"

"Great. What do we know?"

"The hypothesis was, when I handled certain objects, I could see things about the prior owner. With the ring, I saw the owner's death."

"Do you think the dress's owner is still alive?"

I shook my head. "No idea. I'm afraid wedding dress fashion is way outside my area of expertise. This dress could have been worn two hundred years ago or last Friday."

"I don't suppose it has an invitation in the pocket?"

"Wedding dresses, sadly, don't have pockets," I said. "Neither, for that matter, do most of my pants. Olive would probably know the time period, if I could talk to her."

Rusty stepped back, examining the dress critically. "It's turning yellow in places. I'd guess that it's pretty old."

"But what does that mean?"

"If the dress's original wearer died, then you're seeing something other than deaths. That information could be useful."

I sighed. "But for now, we have more questions than answers. Here, unbutton me so I can take it off. I need to try something else."

The two of us searched the store, looking for any items that might give us more information. I wrapped a gorgeous purple boa around my neck. Immediately, my ears filled with swing music. I grabbed Rusty and started moving my hips. He laughed, but after a moment followed my lead. We danced until the song ended and restarted, when I realized that this interlude might last forever if I didn't take the boa off. Too bad. Fun, but not getting us any closer to finding Earl's murderer. Some objects told me nothing.

At least it seemed clear that I wasn't just seeing people's final moments. Maybe I was seeing powerful memories, moments with special meaning to the owner, rather than just the ends of their lives.

At one point I shook a baby's rattle. Instantly, cramping overtook my body. I bent forward, gasping for breath. Everything hurt. I'd never felt such intense pressure in my abdomen. A scream escaped me.

Rusty raced over and yanked the rattle out of my hand. "What happened?"

"I think I just went into labor."

"Whoa."

Yeah, that about summed it up. I couldn't even respond, still doubled over with the spasms. He helped me over to the table, settling me into the chair as if I were made of china. Slowly, the pain subsided.

Finally, I said, "If I ever have kids, remind me to ask for an epidural."

"Check. Sorry. Let's try something else."

After that, I needed a break. It had been two hours, and I was exhausted. Rusty was enthusiastic, and it was great to have someone I could share things with, but he didn't know any more about any of this stuff than I did. We'd tested and retested our hypothesis, but I still didn't know how to call a vision from an object if it didn't send me one.

Only one thing was clear: I needed Olive.

14

About an hour after Rusty left the shop, Sam showed up to relieve me. He looked shell-shocked. Like he'd woken up this morning and gone to work as usual, never suspecting that he'd have to drive a hundred miles to visit his mother in jail after she'd been arrested for a murder she didn't commit. My heart went out to the poor guy. The man he loved like a father was dead, and police thought his mother did it. I ached to give him a hug, but we were virtual strangers and he was my boss's son. It would be too weird.

"Hey," I said as he dropped into a seat at the table by the register. "How's your mom?"

"Scared. Confused. Pretty much the way you'd feel if you were in jail on suspicion of murder."

Fair enough. I would be all those things but also livid at the injustice. "I don't understand what happened. Why would anyone want to frame your mother?"

He sighed. "Probably the most obvious reason is so they don't get caught?"

My mind went back to the conversation between Mayor Banister and Sheriff Matthews. There were many reasons to arrest *someone*. Although I barely knew her, I didn't really think the Mayor was the one who killed Earl. She was too enraged at the idea of someone committing such a heinous act in *her* town. Did she make the Sheriff plant the evidence, or did someone else frame Olive?

Why go after her, of all people? "Does your mom have any enemies? Anyone who would want to see her take the fall?"

Sam took so long thinking about the question, I almost repeated it. "I don't think so. Thelma seems convinced Mom is guilty, but I don't know that she'd set her up."

"This whole thing smells rotten," I said. "I wish I'd found the broken lock on the back door sooner. Then at least there would be a record of a break-in. Now if we report it, it looks like we broke the lock ourselves to explain how Earl's pan got in the store."

"Yeah. I'll take some pictures, just in case, but fix it myself."

"Thanks. The other thing is, Sheriff Matthews found that pan in like two minutes. He must've known right where it was. It should've taken hours to search the entire store."

Sam looked around the store for a long moment before replying. Not wanting to rush his thought process, I waited. Then he said, "You're right. Virtually anything could be hidden in this place. Aside from the fact that the shelves and drawers are overflowing, there are at least a dozen trunks, plus a bunch of armoires."

"Fourteen trunks, seven armoires." I blushed at his inquiring glance. "I counted them while dusting earlier. We didn't have any customers."

"Heh. I used to do that." A dreamy look came over him, as if remembering the old days of working here with his mother. Pain lanced me in the gut. It must be hard for him to be here, knowing she was in jail. Heck, it was hard for me, and I barely knew her.

That reminded me, I needed to get going if I wanted to finish my investigating before dinner. But first, "Did you meet the lawyer? Jake Something?"

"Yeah, he showed up just as I was leaving. Mama and Mom were going to talk to him together. The lawyer wants her to take a lie detector test, but she doesn't want to."

"Lie detectors are bad science," I said. "Anyone gets nervous being hooked up to machines and interrogated."

"Yeah. And everyone's got things to hide." Our eyes met, and in that moment, I was certain he knew exactly what Olive was hiding, not just from the police, but from most of the town. The answer was written all over his face.

It wasn't my place to ask. If I was wrong, Olive would never forgive me for telling her son about her powers. Once we found the real murderer, I'd urge her to have a long talk with her family. Right around the time I talked to mine.

"You're a good son."

"Thanks. She's a great mom." He sighed. "I don't want to keep you. I'm sure you've got better things to do than hang around here all night."

In truth, the thought of hanging around the best-looking guy I knew on a Friday evening sounded a lot more exciting than my usual weekend plans. We could get to know each other and I could comfort him...Unfortunately, I had things to do.

I didn't want him to think I was blowing him off, though, even if it was completely inappropriate to flirt with someone right after their mom got arrested for murder. "I'd stay, but I have plans with Kevin and Kyle later. See you tomorrow?"

"Yeah. Do you mind opening?"

Even if I did, I'd never say so. "No problem."

Part of me wished he'd asked me to stay, but truly, I had places to be.

First stop: Olive.

I'd hoped Officer Matthews would be on duty at the police station when I arrived, but no such luck. When I shut my umbrella and entered the front door, the sheriff stood at the front counter. An open door led to an office, probably his. Behind him were two desks: one so clean it might be unoccupied, and the other looking like a hurricane hit it.

On this side of the counter, talking to Sheriff Matthews, I found the last person in town I wanted to see: Thelma Reyes. Part of me still blamed her for Olive's arrest, even though her rumor-spreading shouldn't have an impact on law enforcement. Mayor Banister was at least as much to blame, but Thelma made an easier target for my frustration.

That woman showed up everywhere. She really took her job as town busybody seriously. Did she have powers, too? Like the ability to teleport? For the first time I wondered if she had a job or if soap opera stars made enough to retire for life in their late forties. My first instinct was to turn around and come back later. But then something hit me. Like a vision, but more a flash of a memory.

Thelma Reyes, using a massive handkerchief with the letter T on the front. A handkerchief identical to the one that made me slip outside of Missing Pieces, hours after police found the supposed murder weapon inside the store. A broken lock on the door. The woman who claimed to be "practically engaged" to Earl, despite evidence to the contrary. She had access to his house. And her only alibi was that she was alone in her kitchen, cooking. She looked guiltier by the second.

I gave Thelma a polite hello, then turned to Sheriff Matthews.

"Nice to see you again, Aly," he said. "My nephew tells me you didn't vote for me."

Why did everyone fixate on that? My face flamed. "Um, well, no. I was still in California. Look, but if you clear Olive's name, I promise to vote for you in the next election."

"Are you offering to give me your vote if I free an accused murderer?"

Beside me, Thelma gasped. Great. Now on top of telling the whole town that Olive killed Earl, everyone would think I was trying to bribe the sheriff into setting her free. A pretty pathetic bribe, too. My vote surely couldn't be worth much.

"Relax, Thelma, I'm joking." Sheriff Matthews said. "Did you need anything else?"

"No, thank you. I have to go." Thelma sighed. "My afternoon shows have already started. I've been too upset to watch, but now that my darling Earl's killer is behind bars, maybe I'll be able to focus."

In an effort not to tell her off, I bit my tongue so hard I tasted blood. Gross.

Sheriff Matthews turned to me as Thelma slowly riffled through her bag, presumably looking for her keys. "How can I help you?"

"I'm here to see Olive," I said. Preferably without Thelma within a thirty-block radius.

As soon as the door closed behind her, I said, "Sheriff Matthews, have you tried talking to Wendy Diaz about Earl's murder?"

"Wendy? Why do you ask?" His face turned red. "Oh, Aly. Now I know why that name is familiar. I thought it was because Doug interviewed you at the store the other day, but you're the one who's been interfering in my investigation."

A chill went down my spine. How he could possibly

know that I'd been asking questions? That didn't count as interfering, did it? I just wanted to prove Olive's innocence. It wasn't like I was planting evidence or faking DNA test results.

"Interfering? I don't know what you're talking about."

"So you're not poking around town, asking questions, interviewing people?"

Oh, crap. Yes, I was doing that. Lying to police felt a lot weirder than lying to Wendy and Benji, but I didn't have a choice. I straightened up and lifted my head. "I'm doing research—."

"Stop right there," he said. "I don't know how they do things in California, but in upstate New York, most people don't get an associate's degree in biology before moving on to broadcast journalism."

My cheeks grew warm. It never occurred to me that anyone might look into my story. "I'm not allowed to change my major?"

"You are," he said. "But if you did, then Organic Chemistry, Physics II, Molecular Genetics, and Advanced General Biology Seminar seem like an odd course load for the upcoming semester."

Suddenly, I felt lightheaded. All I wanted was to help Olive. One white lie didn't seem like a big deal at the time. Now I'd gotten caught lying to the sheriff. He was going to lock me up and throw me back there in jail with her and—

"Relax. You look like you're going to throw up."

"I might," I whispered.

"Good. Consider this your only warning. Butt out."

"I'm sorry," I said. "I just want to find out what happened."

"We know what happened," he said. "We have a suspect

in custody, as you're aware. The murder weapon was found in her possession, and she had motive."

"Olive didn't do it. She was framed." I started to detail the evidence, but he cut me off.

"Well, if she didn't, then it's my job to find the truth," he said. "The police force has a small budget since last year's cuts, but we don't need a teenager risking her life solving murders."

"I'm twenty-one-years old. I'm not a child. Something's not right," I insisted. "I ran into Wendy at the bowling alley last week, and she lied about where she was when Earl died."

A bark of laughter escaped him. "You think Wendy killed Earl? She barely weighs a buck twenty, soaking wet. How could she hit anyone hard enough to kill them?"

"Force equals mass times velocity. Anyone could kill with the right object." My cheeks grew warm. "Except, you know, Olive."

"Nice try, kid. I know you're upset about your boss, but I promise, Wendy didn't have anything to do with this."

"So you've talked to her?"

"Not that it's any of your business, but I personally confirmed her alibi."

What alibi? That she was walking Fluffykins at the time of the murder? He had to be lying, unless he spoke dog. Did anyone in this town ever tell the truth about anything? My head was starting to spin from all the lies and misdirection.

Instead of banging my head against the counter, I reminded the sheriff that I'd come to talk to Olive. He apologized and went to unlock the side door leading to the jail. "Right this way."

A large holding cell took up about three quarters of the room. A wooden chair faced the bars, reminding me of *The*

Silence of the Lambs. We apparently didn't have anyone else in jail at the moment. The cell was empty, except for one bench along the far wall where Olive sat, staring at the floor.

My poor friend looked like sh—well, she looked like she'd been in a jail cell all day. Old makeup smeared under her eyes, hair limp and greasy. This was the first time I'd seen her without lipstick, and it made her seem naked.

She opened her arms when she saw me, pushing her hands through the bars. I went right in for a hug, despite Sheriff Matthews's protests and the metal digging into the side of my face. Her familiar scent enveloped me.

"Make room for the Holy Ghost, ladies," he said.

"You think I'm going to slip her a weapon or maybe a dose of arsenic?" I asked.

He snorted. "I'm just saying—stay apart. I need to see your hands at all times. You two can talk for a bit, but I'll be right on the other side of that door, watching on that camera."

"You can't record our conversation." Thank you, *Aly McBeal* reruns.

"It's video only, missy," Sheriff Matthews retorted. "You've got ten minutes."

Begrudgingly, I left Olive's side to settle into the hard, wooden chair. She remained at the bars. Finally, the sheriff left us alone.

"Are you okay? Really?" I asked as soon as the door closed behind him.

She nodded. "Maria came by to see me earlier, then Sam, as you know. They both know I'm innocent. As long as I have my family, I'll get through this."

"What about the lawyer? Jake Something from Willow Falls?"

"Oh, sweetie, I appreciate the offer, but I don't need a lawyer. The truth will prevail."

"Olive, you're in jail. You're going to be charged with murder."

"Pfft. Everyone knows I didn't do it. Just because I didn't like Earl doesn't mean I killed him."

Okay, sure, not liking a person didn't mean she killed him. Lots of people didn't like each other. But having an argument with the victim mere hours before he was killed certainly gave police reason to suspect her. Especially when they'd found the murder weapon in her store, and she freely admitted not liking him. I didn't know much about law enforcement, but if "everyone" knew she was innocent, she probably wouldn't be in jail.

"They found Earl's skillet in the store," I pointed out. "That looks pretty bad."

"Do you think I did it, too?" Her voice rose with each word.

"Of course not! I'm saying, use your lawyer. Don't take a chance on representing yourself. Maybe Jake can get you out of here until the trial."

She shook her head. "I'm afraid not. The judge is in Willow Falls today, so the arraignment is scheduled for Monday morning. But Jake said bail is almost never allowed in murder cases. There's too much incentive for the accused to run."

"But your life is here! Your wife, and your business—"

"None of which I'll ever see again if I'm convicted," she said gently. "It's okay. I'm confident the truth will come out soon enough."

"I hope you're right." With a glance at the door, I cleared my throat, then said, "Hey, listen, something weird happened."

"Weirder than police finding the murder weapon inside the store and arresting me for a murder I didn't commit?"

"Touché. But also, yes."

She leaned toward me, voice lowered to ensure that Sheriff Matthews couldn't hear. "You had another vision!"

"Several." I nodded. "Not about Earl, though."

Quickly, I explained about drinking from the tea set and the experiments with Rusty. "I don't know what's happening, but I can't control it! It's so frustrating. How am I supposed to get you free if I don't know what I'm doing?"

"Take a deep breath. You've made a lot of progress in a short time. Already you've discovered that you're more likely to have a vision if you're using an item rather than just touching it, right?"

"Right."

"And you're finding that you're only having visions of important events, right?"

"Mostly. The swing dancing was fun, but not exactly earth-shattering."

"True. Maybe that moment meant more to the person who experienced it the first time."

An excellent point, so I nodded. "I also don't know how to control the visions. It's totally inconsistent. I've never had anything hit me while driving Kevin's car. Or, you know, using his plates and sitting on his furniture all day, every day."

"Maybe the prior owner has to be dead for you to get something off an object?"

"Maybe," I said. "I don't know much about the people I saw. I felt one woman giving birth, but I didn't have any sense of what happened to her later."

"It's also possible that your powers will get stronger with time. What you've seen so far are very powerful memories.

For the most part, sitting or eating or riding in a car is pretty mundane, not likely to leave an impression. In time, you'll probably have more control. You may even be able to turn it on and off with practice."

I would *love* to be able to turn this power off. But choosing when to turn it on would also be useful. At the moment it felt like someone had handed me a powerful flashlight that only worked in brightly-lit rooms.

"I hope you're right. Meanwhile, I need to get my hands on that skillet. That should tell me who wielded it, right?"

"It may not be that simple," she said. "If the killer grabbed the skillet, passed a mirror, and then hit Earl, sure. But otherwise, when you've had these visions, have you gotten a sense of whose vision it was?"

"No." I sighed heavily. "What a useless power."

"Stop that! It's not useless. When I get out of here, we'll work on making you stronger. But meanwhile, you may get something else that helps. A flash of jewelry, rings. Even the fingernails may give you an idea who we're dealing with."

"Especially if it's Thelma."

Olive said, "Exactly. She wouldn't be caught dead leaving the house without a perfect manicure."

An unfortunate choice of words, but accurate.

"It's all moot unless I can get to the skillet, anyway," I said. "Without a coroner's report, we don't even know it was the murder weapon. Only that it went missing from Earl's house after he died."

"It's not the murder weapon," Olive said.

"How can you be so sure?"

"That pan was seasoned when they found it."

I looked at her blankly. "And...?"

"You're not a cook, are you?"

I couldn't tell her that a three-year-old helped prepare most of my meals. "Not really."

"Cast iron is great because you can bake oil into it to make the surface non-stick. They call that seasoning. You don't scrub cast iron. If you do, it loses the non-stick quality. You also don't sell a used cast iron pan with an inch of seasoning on it. Any pan sold in Missing Pieces should be smooth and clean."

Realization dawned on me. "So you're saying the pan they found hidden in the store still had its coating?"

"Right," she said. "It didn't look like it had been washed recently. If it actually killed Earl, there would be evidence still on it. Hair, blood. But there wasn't. We were both standing right there when Doug bagged it."

I was rather impressed she'd taken in any of that while being arrested. Most of my energy had been used for not panicking. "Then what killed him?"

She raised her hands in a shrug. "That's the million-dollar question."

15

W hen I got back to the lobby, Sheriff Matthews was nowhere to be seen. Probably over in the Mayor's office congratulating himself on making a quick arrest, I thought bitterly. Doug sat at one of the desks behind the counter.

He looked up from his phone when I entered. "You ready to sign out?"

"Not quite yet," I said. "I'd like to review the police report, please."

He shook his head slowly. "Aly, I like you. You're smart. You're passionate. And you're making a big mistake here. You've been working at Missing Pieces for what, a week?"

"Three days," I mumbled.

"Is this really the hill you want to die on? I know you want to protect your boss, but all the evidence points at Olive. Let it go."

"If all the evidence really points to her, I'll let the evidence convince me. Come on. I know police reports are available to the public. It's on your website."

"It's not finished yet."

"I'll wait."

"Who says I'm working on it now?"

I waved my arms at the open space. "What else would you be doing? Mediating the dispute over the Changs' cat? There's no crime in Shady Grove."

"There is now," he said.

His tone sobered me, because he was absolutely right. At the end of the day, a man was dead, and I needed to remember that, even though I'd barely known him. It was easy to crack jokes, but the best way to help Earl now was to find the killer and bring them to justice.

"I'm sorry," I said. "This is all so hard to believe. It's murder, you know? But listen, something weird's going on."

I told him about the conversation I'd overheard while lurking outside the Mayor's office, and how it happened very shortly before they'd shown up with the warrant based on the mysterious tip from an "unknown caller."

"That tip was legit," Doug said. "I took it myself."

"Yeah? Who called it in?"

"You know I can't tell you that."

I shook my head. "I think someone planted the skillet and then made the tip. Someone broke into Missing Pieces during the last couple of days. I know it sounds nuts, but I think it was Thelma. I found her handkerchief in the alley."

He shook his head. "You can't just walk around accusing people, Aly."

"But she dropped her handkerchief!"

"That monster!" Doug gasped, then spoke in his normal voice. "Sorry. I appreciate you wanting to help your boss, but unless you bring me something concrete, the case is closed."

"And I get that you need to support your uncle. But where is he now? Why did he only arrest Olive after the mayor told him to get someone? Without a coroner's report or a final police report?"

Doug rubbed his chin thoughtfully. After a long moment, he dropped his head into his hands before looking up at me. "Listen. I thought it was odd that Uncle Tim wanted to review the report before I released it. I'm not saying that I believe you, but I'll take things from here. If you promise to let it drop, to leave the investigation to the professionals, I'll show you the draft before I give it to him."

I would promise no such thing. I said would let the evidence convince me, but that was all. It didn't seem prudent to mention that. "Thank you."

He handed me a few paper-clipped pages and returned to his desk, one eye still on me. "Don't try to leave with that."

As if I could outrun him to the door. Even considering that Doug would have to open the gate separating the lobby from his work area—well, I wasn't stupid. "I promise."

The basic report was fairly straightforward and didn't give much information I didn't already have: they got the nine-one-one call from Thelma a few minutes after six, she seemed distraught, and the ambulance driver confirmed that Earl was dead when they arrived. The preliminary conclusion was that the time of death was around four-thirty, about an hour after Earl left Missing Pieces.

At the bottom of the page, Doug had inventoried the crime scene. Mostly standard kitchen stuff. He noted a hanging pot rack with a full range of cast iron arranged by size. That explained how they'd realized a single pan was missing. I wouldn't know if any one item vanished from my own kitchen, unless it was the toaster. Don't mess with my breakfast. Then the report detailed the items on the table where Earl had been found: feathers, powdered rose thorn, and skink root sitting beside a small, empty cauldron. Also a dagger. Not the ingredients for anything Kyle ever made.

The phone on Doug's desk rang. I glanced up long enough to note that as he answered it, he perched on the edge of his desk, his back to me. *Please let this be a long, long call.*

I flipped the page to the attached images. I hurriedly skipped over the pictures of Earl slumped over the table and moved to the inventory. There. After Earl had been taken away, the final picture zoomed in on his kitchen table. Someone had set it up an awful lot like some of the altars I'd seen online while searching for information on psychics. Was Earl a witch? If so, what type of spell had he been planning to cast before he died? Was that why he'd been so sure the statue of Oshun was fake? Maybe he put a love spell on someone, and it didn't work. If his girlfriend found out, she'd be pretty angry. Especially when she'd spent her entire day making him a romantic meal. Walking in on him would've been a slap in the face.

Funny how easily I accepted that witches were real. There was only one problem: who was the intended target? Was it Julie? She was barely half Earl's age, but a lot of people didn't care about stuff like that.

No way Doug would let me make copies of this report. I glanced up to make sure he was still preoccupied with his call, and then snapped images of the altar with my phone. I didn't have the first clue what to make of these items, but Earl probably bought them locally.

Time to visit the magic shop.

Back on Main Street, Come In For a Spell was thankfully open for the first time I'd ever seen. I didn't know where I would've gone next if it was still closed. Nervously, I stepped over the threshold, worrying that I'd somehow stumbled into a place I shouldn't be.

You're being silly, I told myself. This is a public place and it's open for business.

P is for Plutonium. K is for Potassium. Z is for—

"Hello, there!"

I jumped about a foot at the sound. Looking around, I found a black man with a head full of thin, graying braids that touched his chin. His mouth appeared to be set in a perpetual smile. "Mr. Patel? You work here?"

My neighbor grinned at me. "Please, call me Garrett. My daughter owns this place, but we've been open by appointment only since her divorce. She's in Europe 'finding herself.' It's a good thing you caught me. Rajini still needs to be careful of her bad ankle, and I have my restaurant in Willow Falls."

When I moved in, our babysitter had been the most active sixty-year-old I'd ever met. She'd signed up to run the New York City marathon this year. Her skiing incident a few weeks ago had sidelined her, but I strongly suspected she still intended to race unless someone physically stopped her.

"She's a force of nature," I said. "Kyle adores her."

"And she adores him." He grinned at me. "But you didn't come in to chat. Can I help you find something?"

I hesitated. "I'm wondering what you can tell me about love spells."

"Love spells?" His eyebrows knit together as he frowned at me. "That's dangerous stuff. Love can turn to obsession too easily. If that's what you want, I can't help you."

"It's not for me," I blurted out. "I mean, I'm not trying to perform a love spell. I'm here to do research."

"You helping someone else would make things even more dangerous. The blind leading the blind, as they say."

This wasn't working. I supposed I could feed him the same "taking a podcasting class" line I'd been giving everyone else, but I sensed that if I wanted anything from Garrett, I needed to be straight with him. He was working at his daughter's magic shop, so he must be pretty open-minded.

By the time I finished explaining, the suspicious look on his face had been replaced with one of concern.

"Rajini and Amira are the real experts, but I've been around for a long time. Olive's always been a good customer. Let me see." He moved his glasses down to the tip of his nose and held my phone at arm's-length.

Finally, he shook his head. "No, that's not love spell stuff. Love spells use canary feathers, and these are crow. Crows are too moody for love. Too much discontent. That's not the type of relationship people want. And he'd need rose petals, not thorns. Anyone tried a love spell with this batch of ingredients, they'd scare their intended away."

"Are you sure? Earl was using a fertility goddess."

"Who better than a goddess to help erase feelings of love?"

The words hit me like a thunderbolt. Discontent. Not wanting to get married. An overly amorous partner. Erasing love.

The spell *was* for Thelma.

It just wasn't for love.

16

Living in a small town had its perks. Earl lived on "the other side" of Shady Grove—about two miles from home, a mile or so from Missing Pieces. I could be there soon, sooner if I borrowed Olive's bicycle, which was parked behind the store. She wasn't going to be using it, but just in case, I texted Maria for permission. In an instant, she told me to do whatever I needed. I appreciated her faith in me. Not just Maria, the entire family. With all my heart, I hoped I wouldn't let them down.

There was no way I was going to pick up a used bicycle helmet from the store and put it on my head, so I decided to risk going without. Sure, I might get a ticket or bash my head in. But at least I wouldn't be having hallucinations while traveling across town.

As I rode down Main Street, I remembered Kyle. More specifically, I remembered that Kevin's bowling league had a memorial for Earl tonight. Mrs. Patel was going to give my nephew dinner and watch him until I got off work. I'd promised to bring home a special dessert to make up for not being home as much the past week. The bike came to a screeching halt in front of Let's Bake a Deal, the town bakery. They had delicious baked goods, but unfortunately, as I learned on my first day in town, the owner didn't barter. When I'd pointed out what "making a deal" meant, Tony suggested I sue him for false advertising.

Now that I thought about it, I'd prefer not to go in there, but desperate times. I couldn't carry ice cream cones on a bicycle, the corner store didn't sell fresh baked goods, and I didn't have time to take Kevin's car over to Willow Falls. Four minutes later, I placed a gorgeous chocolate-frosted cake in the basket of Olive's bike before continuing to Earl's house.

Now that I'd decided to break in, I didn't want to wait until tomorrow. For one thing, if I went home and thought about it, I might chicken out. The longer it took to find the killer, the more time poor Olive would sit in jail. Not to mention, since psychic imprints weren't proof, I'd have to convince Sheriff Matthews once I figured out who did it. That would be a fun conversation.

"Hey, Sheriff, I know who killed Earl!"

"Oh, yeah? How?"

"I had a vision. I know what you're thinking, that visions aren't real. And a week ago, I would have agreed with you. Turns out, I'm a psychic."

"There's no such thing as a psychic."

"See, I thought so, too. Always felt like just a normal girl. But I assure you, I really am psychic. Just, you know, a normal psychic. Oh, and I like science."

I'd probably get that MRI I'd been thinking about all week, because Sheriff Matthews would definitely call in the medical professionals. No, I needed to find something concrete, fast.

If I got lucky and the real murder weapon was in Earl's house somewhere, I could use whatever it told me to confront the murderer. Preferably in public, on video, surrounded by heavily armed men and/or martial arts experts.

With every minute that ticked by, I grew more nervous. What exactly did I think I was doing?

Saving a friend, I told myself firmly. *And then celebrating with cake.*

Element number nineteen is potassium. Number twenty is calcium.

Since I didn't want anyone to see me, I turned off the main road into the entrance for the golf course that ran behind Earl's and Thelma's backyards. Kevin had a membership, which meant I could visit any time I wanted. Thanks, Bro. We didn't use it often, but he liked to have a place he could meet wealthier clients who traveled up from the city, and I liked the children's programs that let me hang out by the pool for an hour a day last summer while someone else watched Kyle. I loved that kid with all my heart, but sometimes a girl needed a break.

No one paid any attention to me when I turned onto the path leading to the greens. The actual golfing was closed due to the mountains of snow everywhere, but the club cleared the trails for those weirdos who liked to exercise outside in the winter. I was free to walk or ride along the paths until the club closed when the sun set. Considering it was January, that would be around four o'clock in the afternoon, so there was no time to waste. It was already almost three-thirty.

I made it to the fifth hole before realizing I didn't have the first clue where Earl's house was relative to the golf course or what it looked like. All I knew was what I'd been told: there were trees separating the backyard from the greens. Considering how many trees surrounded the *Shady*

Grove Golf Club—not to mention most of the town—that wasn't terribly helpful.

If they'd left the police tape up, I could probably find Earl's place, but otherwise I was flying blind. This realization brought me to a dead halt, so fast I nearly catapulted over the handlebars. The cake lunged forward, but thankfully, I avoided tragedy by catching it.

A quick text to Sam resolved my problem. He gave me the address, even better, without asking why I wanted it. Between that and Google maps, I soon knew exactly which house belonged to Earl. More importantly, Streetview showed me Thelma's house. It has been painted an eye-searing shade of Pepto-Bismol pink, which made it super easy to find the house next door. I was at least a quarter mile away when I spotted her split-level home.

Unfortunately, houses do not list their addresses on the back, so I didn't immediately know which of Thelma's neighbors' houses to break into. One hundred percent, I didn't want to pick the wrong one. Back to Google. The internet told me that Earl lived in a three-bedroom ranch. The house on the other side of Thelma's was a colonial with a walkout basement. It didn't take long to differentiate between the two.

Since I couldn't pedal through the row of trees, I left Olive's bike on the path and inched toward the line between the properties. It hadn't snowed since Earl died, so I anticipated an easy dash across his back yard to the door. As soon as I exited the trees, my error became really obvious.

It hadn't snowed since Earl passed.

It had, however, snowed on Wednesday morning, while Earl was still alive. The temperature hadn't risen above freezing since. Thirty pristine feet of snow stretched between the bike trail and Earl's back door, meaning the killer hadn't entered the house from the golf course.

It was very apparent from this vantage point that the murderer had exactly two viable options: The first was to go up the driveway, presumably plowed by Earl before he left for work, and follow the path to the front door. I couldn't see the walk, so I had no idea whether it had been cleared. But even if it wasn't, with Sam's visit and packages and mail and grocery deliveries and everything, it would be impossible to even identify one complete set of footprints in the snow, much less figure out who they belonged to. That was a dead end.

Alternatively, the killer could have used the path leading from Thelma's back door to Earl's, which someone had shoveled. That was the path Thelma took when she went to get him for dinner, and they presumably went back and forth often. If that was the entry point, the killer was either Thelma or someone with access to her house.

Then again, this was Shady Grove, where businesses didn't lock their doors at the end of the day. The entire town could have access to Thelma's house for all I knew.

I needed to get into the house. Unfortunately, I couldn't go this way. If Thelma looked out her kitchen window, she'd see a clean line of footprints across the backyard that hadn't been there an hour ago. If she didn't call the police immediately, she'd come to investigate. Either way, I'd have to see someone I preferred to avoid.

With a sigh, I retraced my path out of the golf course, resigned to approach the house from the front and hope no one saw me.

I came to a halt in Earl's driveway a few minutes later. Darkness had started to fall while I cycled around, and he thankfully didn't have automatic lights or motion detectors.

The streetlights already gave me more exposure than I wanted, but there was nothing I could do about it. If I parked the bike behind the garage, it shouldn't be visible from Thelma's house. I knew nothing about Earl's other neighbor, but it was a necessary risk.

I'd made it exactly five steps wheeling the bike up the driveway before a voice stopped me.

"You there! What are you doing?"

A wave of dread hit me at the sound of her voice. I turned slowly, hoping that I'd imagined it. No such luck. Standing on the sidewalk not five feet away, hands on her hips, was Thelma.

17

W hat horrific luck. All I'd wanted was to break into Earl's house, find the murder weapon, trigger a vision that told me exactly who killed him, then go home and watch kiddie movies on the couch with Kyle while we snuggled and ate cake. The perfect evening. I knew there was zero chance I'd manage to get into the house without Thelma's eagle eyes on me unless someone lured her away first, but she shouldn't been at the memorial for at least another hour. Surely she wouldn't have skipped it and given up being the center of attention.

On the other hand, this was a great time to get some information. From what I knew about Thelma, she was happy to talk about anything and everything to anyone who would listen. That might help me.

Unless she killed Earl. At the moment, she was my top (only?) suspect. If she knew Earl had been flirting with Julie, that gave her a strong motive. I didn't want to go anywhere near her. But I also didn't want her to realize why I was here, or how close I (thought I) was to proving that she was a killer. Better to play it cool and leave as soon as possible.

With a smile I hoped looked sincere, I stepped toward her. "Thelma! I'm glad you came home before I left."

"I don't live here." She pointed to the house next door, which to be honest, did look a lot more like the home of a former soap opera star. All ivy and trellises and a rose garden and pink. So much pink. Had I truly been looking for Thelma's house, I should have known it wasn't the fairly nondescript ranch house with a sagging porch and peeling brown paint even if I hadn't seen her place online.

"You mean I almost knocked on the wrong door? How embarrassing. Listen, I came to apologize for the other day at the coffee shop. I was way out of line. Also, I brought you a cake."

Her narrowed eyes widened the smallest crack. "Cake?"

"From Let's Bake a Deal. Vanilla with chocolate frosting." Kyle was going to throw a fit when I came home empty-handed. But if I went to jail for breaking and entering, I wouldn't be coming home at all, so he'd have to get over it.

"Thank you, dear. That's sweet." She sighed. "I've just left Earl's memorial, and I'm beside myself. I'd prefer not to be alone."

Now I felt terrible for my lie. If Thelma was depressed enough to want to hang out with me, she must've really loved Earl. "I know I said this before, but I'm so sorry for your loss."

"Thank you." She sniffled and wiped a tear from her cheek. It occurred to me that this might be the first genuine show of emotion I'd ever seen from her. "Please, please come in."

Snow covered both lawns, so I followed the driveway back down to the sidewalk before heading over to Thelma's house.

"What a beautiful home. I love the color," I lied as I

followed her inside, stamped the snow off my boots, and left them by the doorway.

Thelma took the cake I'd promised my nephew into the kitchen and told me to have a seat on the couch. A moment later she returned carrying a tray with a teapot, cups with saucers, and plates holding two not-big-enough slices of cake. Sometimes Shady Grove felt antiquated, but I loved living in a place where people regularly served tea on trays that also held baked goods. I could get used to this. I made a mental note to buy myself a tea set after I'd gotten a few paychecks. New, of course.

"That was fast!"

"A little secret, dear. Always have a kettle on. You never know when company might drop by. Case in point."

"You're not worried about burning your house down?"

"Oh, heavens no! You're so dramatic." She placed one hand on her chest in a way that left me itching to point out the irony. "Anyway, what can I help you with?"

You could go away and leave me to break into Earl's house to look for clues. When I'd pretended that Thelma was the person I'd come to see, I hadn't thought things through. Like, why I'd want to see someone I barely knew and who kept calling my boss a murderer. Thinking fast, I stuffed a bite of cake into my mouth.

Oh, my goodness, that was amazing. So good. Moist, buttery cake with a creamy chocolate frosting that melted on my tongue. Not helping me figure out what to say, but utterly delicious.

Finally, I decided to play on Thelma's love for being the center of attention. It seemed the best way to get her talking. "I wanted to see how you were doing. Finding Earl must have come as quite a shock."

"Oh, you have no idea." She leaned forward and lowered

her voice to a whisper. "My doctor almost had to prescribe anti-anxiety medication. Can you imagine?"

I cleared my throat. "Research shows that anti-anxiety medication has been extremely eff...Ahem. I mean, this cake is fantastic!"

"Yes, thank you for bringing it."

Now that she was softened up a bit, I decided to see what she would tell me. The trip didn't have to be wasted just because she'd stopped me from getting into Earl's house. As long as Thelma didn't know I suspected her, it should be fine.

"Can you tell me what happened? You went next door for dinner on Wednesday, right?"

She glared at me. "I appreciate the cake, but I know someone digging for gossip when I see it. I may be old, but I'm no old fool."

Oops. So much for easing into things. Not knowing what else to say, I grasped for the excuse I'd given at the bowling alley earlier in the week. "My apologies. I didn't know if you'd talk to me knowing the real reason I'm here. The thing is, I really want to be a true crime podcaster. I'm starting college soon, and one of my classes requires us to follow a real crime. I thought if I picked something both local and personal to me, the teacher would give me a good grade."

"What's a podcast?"

"It's like a radio show, but online." I pulled out the one thing that might get her to help me. "If I use this case for my presentation, you'd be the star of my class. You could even come in to talk to everyone."

"Okay, fine," she said. "I might as well tell you what everyone already knows."

"Thank you. I appreciate it." As long as I didn't have to

actually sign up for a course on podcasting, which I still didn't know if Maloney College offered.

Thelma waved one hand, dismissing my words, then settled into her story. "Earl and I had a date. I spent all day roasting a turkey for him, to celebrate him winning the bowling tournament last week. Roasted turkey is his favorite, and I wanted to make it right away. It's so hard to find something this side of the holidays, you know? Luckily I had one in my freezer downstairs, but it takes days to defrost. You can't rush a turkey."

"What time did you go over there?"

"Right after six," she said. "He was supposed to get here early to set the table, but he hadn't arrived yet. Earl was never late. We always ate at six o'clock sharp. He didn't answer the phone, so I decided to pop over and see what was keeping him."

"Do you have a key?"

She shrugged. "I don't need a key. Earl always left his doors open."

My ears perked up. "Really? Who else knew that?"

"Um...Let's see. The mailman, of course. He left packages inside, out of the snow. The milk delivery boy, the UPS driver, Stacey, his housecleaner..." She continued listing names, ticking them off on her fingers. "Plus all our friends. This isn't New York City. No one locks their doors."

She made a valid, if frustrating, point. If what Thelma said was true, then anyone could have walked in and murdered Earl. My suspect list was essentially everyone within a fifty-mile radius who knew how to open a door. Even Kyle fit that description.

"What did you see when you walked in?"

"There he was. Sitting in his usual spot with his back to the door, head on the kitchen table." She shuddered and wiped her eyes. Poor Thelma. She really did care about Earl. You know, unless she was acting and she was the person who murdered him. I still knew nothing, including whether to trust a word she said. "For a moment I wanted to believe he fell asleep, but then I saw the way his eyes stared into space. I thought he might've suffered a heart attack until I looked down and saw all the blood."

"That's horrible," I said honestly. "What did you do?"

"I screamed. Ran to him. Dropped to my knees."

Reaching over and patting her hand, I reminded myself not to feel too terrible for her. Even if she didn't do it, she still could be the one who set up Olive. Someone had to drop her handkerchief.

"That must've been awful for you," I said.

She nodded. "I didn't want to believe he was dead. I still don't want to believe it."

"I'm so sorry for your loss."

"Thank you." She sniffled and sipped her tea. "I know you don't want to believe Olive killed my Earl, but all the evidence points in that direction."

"I saw their argument, Thelma," I said. "Earl walked in yelling, threw a figurine at the wall behind the cash register, and stormed out. That was it. Olive barely had time to blink. Earl left the store alive."

"Then why did she come here after that?"

"She didn't. The car you saw belongs to Sam, Olive and Maria's son."

She narrowed her eyes at me. "I know what I saw."

"I'm sure you do. The car was here. But did you see Olive in the flesh?"

"Well, no. Just the car."

"That's Sam's Beetle. He has the title they signed over to him when he graduated college."

"So Olive's son did her dirty work!"

I shook my head, trying to hide my exasperation. "No. Sam was dropping some paperwork off, and he was on the road to New York City before two. He would have been long gone by the time Earl came into Missing Pieces. You must've seen the car earlier than you thought, because it wasn't in town at four."

"I think I can tell time. That car was here before I went to the grocery store, and I always do my shopping at three. After my two o'clock show, before the four o'clock show. My three o'clock soap is lovely, of course, but it's often repetitive so I can skip a day without missing anything. Especially if the day's storyline follows that dreadful Viki. I could play her role better with my eyes closed!"

Three? Despite her stream-of-consciousness style, her words sparked something in me. I sat up straighter. "No. No way. I stopped by the Grocery Mart right after I saw Earl at Missing Pieces. If you'd left here at three, we'd have run into each other. You weren't there."

"Grocery Mart?" She tapped one perfectly pink finger-nail against her matching lipstick for a minute. "Right. I suppose I could have been off about the time. Are you sure?"

"Positive. Listen, I know Olive didn't do this. One reason I'm here is, I was hoping you could remember something, anything, that might help me prove her innocence."

She stood up straight and sniffed loudly. "I'm sorry, but there's nothing I can do to help you."

"You didn't see anyone enter Earl's house later in the day?"

"No, but I was finishing up dinner. The last half hour or so is the most important. Brushing butter over the biscuits, mashing the potatoes, pulling the stuffing out of the bird and fluffing it up. It all takes time."

"I understand. Thanks for the tea." Since she wasn't going to tell me anything useful, I might as well go home, get another cake for Kyle, eat the entire thing in one sitting, and then come back to search Earl's house later.

Before doing that, I'd need some way to get Thelma out of the house for a couple of hours. I no longer thought sneaking past her and getting in undetected was an option.

I just had one more question. "Is there anyone else who might have had a motive to hurt him?"

She sighed. "No. Earl was such a lovely man. Everyone adored him."

"Do you know Wendy Diaz?" I lowered my voice. "I heard that Wendy's the number two bowler in the league, behind Earl. When I talked to her, she lied about her alibi. Sheriff Matthews didn't care at all when I told him."

"That's because they were together. Wendy's husband works out of state. She and Tim have been having an affair for years. Every Wednesday afternoon at his place. It's his day off."

Oh. Well, that explained a lot. Including how Sheriff Matthews knew I was asking questions about Earl's death. Darn it. There went my number two suspect. Kyle was moving up the list.

I just needed that stupid murder weapon to tell me once and for all what happened. And I still didn't have the first clue how or where to get it. Even when the coroner's report was released, it would probably conclude that Earl had been killed with a cast iron skillet after the conversation between the sheriff and Mayor Banister. Too bad there was no way for me to get my hands on it without getting seated on Olive's jury. Also, the actual evidence strongly suggested the killer used something else.

"How did you know that?"

"They're the worst-kept secret in town. Everyone knows." Everyone except me, apparently. Was I even a resident of Shady Grove? In the kitchen, a phone rang. "Excuse me. I'll be right back."

After she left, I looked around the room. Although Thelma was significantly younger than my great-grandmother, it appeared that they had the same sense of style. Pink floral paper covered the walls, a lush pink carpet on the floor. How did she keep things so clean? Kyle would destroy this room in thirty seconds flat.

On the mantel, I spotted a familiar-looking figurine. A gold person standing on a black base, leaning backward and holding a giant ball. It stood more than a foot high. Curious, I wandered over to take a closer look. This thing looked like it had been through the wringer. Deep scratches covered most of the inscription, but I could still make out the words "Lead Actress" and a bunch of letters that didn't appear to spell Thelma Reyes. Interesting. I thought she'd never won.

With a glance at the kitchen doorway, I whipped out my phone and googled the year. Apparently, the Daytime Emmy Award for Lead Actress had gone to someone I'd never heard of. Not Thelma, according to the picture.

My fingers itched to find out how this came to be on the mantel in front of me. It was none of my business. It had nothing to do with why I was here or finding out who killed Earl. Probably. But, I mean, he'd been hit with something heavy, and this statuette looked pretty beaten up.

One eye still on the doorway where I expected Thelma to reappear, I hefted the statuette and tested its weight. You could take the girl out of science class, but you couldn't take the science class out of the girl. I'd done about a hundred hours of lab to get my associate's degree. We weighed all kinds of stuff, especially in geology lab. After a while, you tend to get a feel for it.

The statuette probably weighed about six and a half pounds. With the right amount of force, it could absolutely be used to bash someone's head in. And it was so shiny, I could see my face in it. This thing had been polished very recently. Cleaning off blood?

This was one of those moments where my newfound powers were both a blessing and a curse. If I could trigger a vision, I might be able to find out if the award had been used to kill Earl.

Alas, I did not know how to do that. But I had to try.

First, I addressed the figure sitting atop the base. "Tell me your secrets!"

Nothing happened. Thelma's voice carried from the kitchen, letting me know that her phone call continued, but she could wrap it up at any moment. I tried rubbing it, but since it wasn't a magic lamp and there was no genie inside, that didn't work at all. Leaning forward, I kissed the statue's tiny face. Nope, that wasn't it.

Finally, desperately, I hoisted it up in front me, grinned as broadly as I could, and said to absolutely no one, "I'd like to thank the Academy."

Aha! The room shifted around me.

I stood at a podium, clutching the statue, gazing out at a sea of faces. Looking down, I discovered that I wore a low-cut pink-sequined evening gown and the highest heels I'd ever seen. Good things my visions didn't require me to walk anywhere.

My mouth opened, and a voice I recognized as Thelma's spoke. "I'm so sorry to tell you all that Kim couldn't be here tonight, but I am thrilled to accept this award on her behalf."

Heh. The sudden vision made me like Thelma a bit more. It took guts to steal someone else's Emmy after accepting it for them. The list of suspects would be one. You had to be very extra to then scratch their name off the metal and display the award on your mantel like your own.

On the other hand, if Thelma had used the Emmy to kill Earl, chances were that moment would be the one sent to me instead of the moment she took possession. So either she wasn't the killer or she'd used something else.

With a sigh, I set the award back on the mantel. My eyes landed on Thelma's open purse sitting on the chair beside the fireplace. Did I dare? What would happen if she caught me going through her stuff?

She had left me alone.

She was definitely a thief.

She might be a killer.

She wouldn't be on the phone much longer.

This could be my only chance to find a clue.

I reached for her purse and grabbed the first item sitting on top: her checkbook. I hadn't seen one of these since my mom taught me how to do a budget in the fourth grade. One thing I remembered, though, was that a lot of people kept carbon copies of written checks for their records.

With a glance at the door and crossed fingers, I opened the book to see where Thelma had been spending her money. I didn't know what I expected to find—"for murder" written in the subject line?

The first check had been written to the grocery store in Willow Falls on Wednesday. Fascinating. She'd spent thirty-one dollars and forty-one cents. Pi! The second check was from the same day, written to a Doctor Tom.

Hmmm. Thelma hadn't mentioned visiting the doctor. She probably thought it was none of my business. She'd be right, but that didn't stop me from googling. When his website filled the screen, I stifled a gasp. Doctor Graham

Tom, specialist in plastic surgery. I knew she didn't look her age.

Not exactly what I'd hoped to find, but still interesting. The carbon copy before that was from the first, written to the phone company. No surprises there. All were in sequence, so nothing appeared to be missing.

As I replaced the checkbook in her purse, something crinkled under my fingers. A receipt from the grocery store. A-ha! What time did she write that check? My eyes skimmed the page, widening to note that she'd purchased a pre-roasted turkey, hot stuffing, and rolls from the bakery. Home-cooked meal, my foot. Thelma certainly had her secrets, but was being a killer among them?

Then I found the time stamp. Almost five o'clock.

Willow Falls was at least forty minutes away. The police estimated the time of death to be around four-thirty. If Thelma was buying this stuff at five, she must've gone to Earl's house right after she got back. He had to have been dead when she entered his house.

The good news was, I hadn't been sharing my nephew's cake with a killer. The bad news was, at this rate, Olive would never be free.

18

By the time I finally got home, I felt like I'd run three emotional marathons. Thelma didn't kill Earl with her (stolen) Emmy. She wasn't even in town when he died, but she wasn't likely to appreciate having to tell anyone where she'd been. She seemed to really love him, though.

I did learn that Wendy was sleeping with Sheriff Matthews, which explained a lot. But I hadn't gotten inside Earl's house, and I didn't love the idea of sneaking back in the middle of the night. Especially because with my luck, Thelma would use her uncanny sixth sense to spot me and insist I come in for a nightcap.

Theoretically, I could call Rusty and ask him to take me inside. But something about asking the next of kin to help me look for the murder weapon didn't sit right, even after our afternoon of vision-testing. Also, if I found what I was looking for, the thought of him watching me relive his uncle's death was cringe-inducing. Not gonna happen. There had to be another way.

Kyle came racing up to the kitchen door when I entered,

with as much energy as if it wasn't ten minutes past his bedtime. "Aly! Cake time?"

I shot a guilty glance at my brother, who looked up from the table where he sat typing away on his laptop. "I, um, may have promised Kyle a treat."

Kevin smiled. "It's fine. I told him we could wait up. Although I was going to call it if you weren't back in another ten minutes or so."

"Sorry. I guess it's a good thing I've got dessert." After leaving Kyle's cake with Thelma, I'd stopped on the way home and gotten ice cream after all. At least in January, I didn't have to worry about it melting on the way home.

"Yay!" He jumped up and down clapping while I got bowls from the cupboard. Without waiting for me, Kyle yanked the silverware drawer open, grabbed three spoons, and ran to the table. Carrying everything else, I followed.

"What'd you get?" Kevin asked.

"Caramel fudge chunk for us, vanilla for Kyle." Kids had no taste at all. Ah, well. More for me.

Opening the cartons, I quickly scooped everything into bowls and handed them out around the table. You've got to love Northeastern winters—the ice cream was harder from sitting in the basket of Olive's bike than it had been when I pulled the cartoons out of the freezer case.

Kyle made airplane noises as his spoon swooped through the air. Kevin and I both watched him, absorbed in our own thoughts. It was nice to have family time together, especially after the frenzied week we'd both had. Once my classes started, I wouldn't be home before bedtime most nights.

"I hear you taught my son a new word this week."

Our morning at the bookstore felt like a month ago, but

the look on my brother's face brought it all rushing back. Grrr. Stupid Brad. "Sorry."

"No worries. I was a little surprised when Kyle asked if I'd m-u-r-d-e-r-e-d anyone, but we've moved on."

A bark of laughter escaped me. Oh, man.

"When do you want to go buy your car?" Kevin asked. "Classes start soon, right?"

"Ten days. I can't believe it." It didn't seem right to go car shopping while my boss sat in jail awaiting trial for murder. "Next weekend?"

"You don't think that's cutting it too close?"

I shrugged. "That gives me a week to figure out what car I want online and get pre-approved for a loan. My generation doesn't buy cars the same way as yours."

"Ouch," Kevin said. "What a way to talk to the person you need to co-sign."

"Good thing you love me." I blew him a kiss. "Seriously, I'm waiting for my first paycheck. The keyword is 'cosign,' not 'buy for me.'"

"Got it. Next week it is." He paused. "I'll get the spare car seat out of storage."

The one that had been in Katrina's car when she died. We'd returned her leased vehicle shortly before the move, and the seat went into the basement. I'd almost forgotten about that storage space—we didn't have basements in my part of California. Suddenly, I wondered what else of my sister-in-law's was down there.

Kyle looked up from his now-empty dish. "More, please?"

"No more, buddy. Time for bed." Kevin stood and walked with my nephew toward the stairs. I watched him thoughtfully.

My brother had never spoken about the day his wife

died. Her obituary said only that she passed, but didn't go into details. There was no point when we didn't know much. After I moved in, I'd chalked Kevin's silence up to grief. After all, I didn't want to relive the worst moment of my life by telling the story over and over, and nothing close to losing a spouse ever happened to me.

But now, it had been over a year. In many ways, Kevin was moving on. He seemed lighter and happier. He slept better, he laughed more. He wasn't dating, but that could take time.

To be fair, I didn't know how long it took to recover from this type of loss. But talking about it might help. Especially now that Earl's death had to be bringing up a lot of thoughts and feelings. Losing a bowling team member obviously wasn't the same as a wife, but still. Better not to let things fester.

When Kevin returned downstairs and settled onto the couch to do some work, I grabbed two mugs of hot cocoa and handed him one. "Hey. How you holding up?"

"Fine. Why?"

"Losing someone unexpectedly can be hard."

"Let me stop you right there. I barely knew Earl. We were bowling acquaintances."

"I wasn't talking about Earl."

At that, Kevin's head shot up. "I'm fine, Aly."

"Are you? Are you really?" I leaned forward. "You never talk about Katrina. Not to Kyle, not to me. By moving here, you've isolated yourself from all your old friends. But also..." I gestured around the room. "Where is Katrina in this house?"

"What are you talking about? I donated her clothes before we moved."

"Right. I understand that. But her fingerprints were all

over the old place. She picked out the paint, the furniture, the décor. Everything."

"We have a three-year-old," he said. "I can't exactly leave knick-knacks all over."

That was a fair point, and I said so. "Okay, but pictures? Do you want Kyle to grow up not knowing what his mother looked like?"

"I have pictures. They're just not out." When he looked up at me, tears shone in his eyes. I hadn't seen him cry since the funeral.

"I'm so sorry. I get that it's painful, but I think it would help to talk."

"There's nothing to talk about," he said shortly. "She's gone. I wasn't home when it happened, I couldn't save her, and that's that."

I studied the side of his shuttered face, marveling at how I didn't realize he was still in so much pain. Clearly, Katrina's death hurt him very badly. For the first time, I realized that he felt responsible, but why? Because he wasn't home when she died? He had a job. No one blamed him for being at work in the middle of a Tuesday afternoon. They'd lived in a giant house in one of the richest suburbs in the tristate area. Local police spent more time mediating PTA disputes than solving crimes. Murder was practically unheard of.

If only we had something of Katrina's lying around, I could try to trigger a vision. But I didn't have any idea where to start. To date, none of the things in this house had spoken to me, and Katrina owned or used almost everything. Kevin got rid of a lot of her stuff when she died, but he kept the furniture, the dishes. Stuff you don't replace while in mourning. All of her clothes were donated before the move, but he must have kept something somewhere.

Downstairs? I didn't have a lot of reason to use the basement. It contained the old car seat, like he said. Kyle's old crib, the high chair, and clothes he'd outgrown. But suddenly I wondered if I'd find anything of Katrina's behind all the baby stuff.

The one thing I knew: until Kevin dealt with losing his wife, he wouldn't truly be able to move on. If he wouldn't talk about what happened, I needed to figure it out on my own so he could heal. It was the only way he could ever be happy again.

There had to be something here. My eyes moved around the room, lingering on every object. Furniture, tables, dishes, a clean mantel...and the side table beside the stairs, hanging under a now-empty spot on the wall.

"Hey, Kev? What happened to the mirror?"

"Mirror?"

"Yeah. Giant mirror, black and silver twisty things on the frame. Looked expensive. Heavy."

"Oh, right," he said absently. "Kyle broke it playing ball inside. Just like I always tell him not to."

Darn. That mirror had to have belonged to Katrina. No way my brother picked it out. Anyway, in front of where the mirror should have been a huge wooden base with a gold-painted cup on top stood on the table. It looked a little too nice to be one of Kyle's art projects, but not by much. Large red characters spelled out "#3" on one side. It hadn't been there when I left the house this morning, because I absolutely would have remembered seeing it.

"What's that?" I asked.

"My bowling trophy," he said proudly. "Our team came in fourth, but I took third place overall. Scored a personal best."

"Oooh, fancy! My brother, the bowling star."

"'Star' is a stretch, but I do enjoy it." He chuckled. "What about you? How are you doing with all of this? Working for an accused murderer can't be easy."

I sighed. "This is all so surreal. A week ago, I was unemployed, sitting here, watching Netflix original movies and trying out Kyle's caramel-chocolate popcorn balls. Now I'm helping run an antique store while trying to solve the crime my boss was accused of committing." *Oh, and I have psychic powers, but it's cool. I don't know how to use them yet.*

Immediately, I wished I could pull my words back. He latched onto that last sentence at the same moment I realized my mistake. "What do you mean, 'trying to solve'? Aly, you know they have professionals to do this type of thing, right? Trained individuals with self-defense skills and weapons and backup?"

"Yes, of course."

"Objection. Non-responsive."

That was the trouble with living with a lawyer. They knew when you were lying, and they used jargon to point it out. Feeding him the same line I'd given everyone else wouldn't work: my brother knew darn well what my major was and that true crime shows freaked me out.

"I just want to help," I said weakly.

"Help. *How*?"

I hesitated as long as I could. As a lawyer, Kevin would hate my plan to break into Earl's house. Although, in my defense, it had completely failed. As my brother, he would hate the idea of me looking into Earl's murder by myself, what with my zero knowledge about anything related to the law or crime or catching murderers. Unfortunately, as both a lawyer and my brother, he also knew when I was hiding something.

The look on my face must've spoken volumes because

he raked his fingers through his hair. "Geez, Aly. Is there anything else endangering your life I should know about?"

"No." My newfound psychic abilities probably wouldn't put my life in danger, and he definitely didn't need to know about them. Avoiding the question, I focused on his trophy. It was bigger than I would've expected. So big, to be honest, I didn't know where we'd put the thing. It was ugly, too. It might look great in the back of Kyle's closet, underneath the spare bedding. But was it heavy?

I hefted it up, weighing it with my arms. Probably about eight pounds. Heavier than Thelma's stolen Emmy. What a waste of wood and metal. Then I swung it in a circle.

"What are you doing?"

"Earl was hit from behind with something heavy. The newspaper article doesn't mention what the murder weapon was, and there's no coroner's report yet. This is big and heavy." An impact hard enough to kill someone would likely splinter the wood, but it could work. And Wendy would have a matching trophy. Sheriff Matthews swore he'd confirmed her alibi, and Thelma said they would've been together.

Would the sheriff lie to protect Wendy? Would Thelma?

"Put that down. This isn't a TV show, you're not Bones, and there's an actual killer on the loose."

I sighed. "Look, I just want Earl's family to know the truth. If someone could give you answers about Katrina, wouldn't you want them to try?"

He froze, and I worried that I'd pushed too far. Sure, we were closer than we'd been a year ago, but this was his wife. Finally, he spoke in a low, quiet voice. "Okay, fine. I will help you reason through this. But I never want to hear you mention Katrina's death again. She's gone. We have no way of knowing who did it. Police have no leads, and too much time has passed. Rehashing the details won't bring her back."

Since getting Olive out of jail was currently the most pressing matter, I didn't argue. But I also crossed my fingers behind my back. "Deal. Let's look at this trophy again. What do you think?"

"You're right. If a person were hit with one of these just right, they might die from the injury."

"How many were there? Does Benji believe in participation trophies for everyone?"

He snorted. "That's an emphatic no. There were three. Me, Earl, and Wendy. But they weren't here on Wednesday Benji was unpacking the box when I arrived for tonight's practice. Said the shipment had just come in."

"Oh, right. Never mind." I shook my head.

"You knew that?"

"I asked about them yesterday when I went to talk to question...I mean...talk to Wendy."

His eyes glittered. "Aly. This is a job for the police."

"But the police aren't doing anything! They locked Olive up and declared the case closed. They don't even have the real murder weapon." I relayed what Olive had told me about the pan, and he nodded along.

"That's good. Very good. Olive's lawyer will point out the holes in the case against her. That's his job, as you know. Police have their own job, which is to follow leads and investigate the evidence."

"Will they actually look for the real murder weapon?"

"Just because they haven't found it yet doesn't mean they didn't try. The first lead was the cast iron skillet. If that doesn't pan out—no pun intended—they'll keep looking. I'm sure you know that most people don't carry murder weapons around on them. It probably got destroyed or thrown away. This can take a while."

"Hold on." Obviously I knew that—I'd had the same thought at Thelma's house. But Kevin's words made something itch in the back of my mind. "Wait. Say that again."

"Which part? Stay out of this?"

I narrowed my eyes at him. "You know that's not what I meant."

"I said that most murderers don't leave the weapon lying around where anyone can find it. They get rid of it."

The itch was getting stronger. "Like throwing it out with the trash?"

"That's one option. There are dozens. What are you getting at?"

The longer I thought about it, the more the missing pieces fell into place. All of a sudden, I knew who killed Earl.

19

A broken trophy. Jealousy.

"Aly?" My brother's voice cut into my thoughts. "What's going on? You're just staring at my trophy."

"The murder weapon. I finally figured it out."

He made an impatient noise. "I assure you, I didn't use my trophy to kill Earl."

"I know that!" I resisted the urge to stomp my foot and insist he take this conversation seriously. "If I thought it was you, would I say so? Listen. When I was at the bowling alley yesterday, I knocked a trash can over on the way out."

"Our parents should have named you Grace."

"They should've named you Kelvin. Oh, wait," I snapped. Sibling taunting was an uncontrollable reflex. I took a deep breath. "The trash can fell over. Something made of wood and metal fell out. Something that looked an awful lot like this trophy. But it was in pieces, and that was before Benji said the trophies arrived, so I didn't look closely."

Kevin leaned back against his chair and tapped his chin

thoughtfully. "Are you sure it looked like this trophy when you were at the bowling alley?"

"Yeah. I didn't think much of it at the time. I mean, I don't usually examine trash, and it was all messed up. I thought it was old, because Benji said this year's hadn't come in yet. But it does look the same. What did last year's trophies look like?"

"We didn't have trophies last year. Tournament cancelled."

"Huh. Maybe an extra?"

"There weren't any extra. Benji only ordered three," he reminded me. "Mine, Wendy's, and Earl's."

"Did Wendy pick up her second-place trophy this evening?"

"Yeah. After the memorial."

"Did you see Earl's?"

Kevin shook his head. "I assumed Benji would give it to Thelma at some point, since they were dating. Or Earl's brother."

Rusty's father. Who probably had zero interest in a giant block of wood with a painted metal cup nailed to the top.

"What if Benji didn't give Earl's trophy to anyone? What if that's the same one I spotted in the trash when I was at the bowling alley? Do you think it's possible that Benji went to deliver it to Earl's house, they argued for some reason, and Benji hit him? Wendy said they were supposed to be delivered on Tuesday."

"That would explain how it got broken," he said. "But what would they be arguing about? Earl's been one of We All Fall Down's best customers for years."

For a long moment, I considered everything I knew about Benji. Okay, a short moment. The list wasn't that long.

I remembered the way he looked at Thelma, the way he told me to leave the coffee shop because I was upsetting her. Olive telling me that he'd had a crush on Thelma for years. And the handkerchief. T for Turner, not T for Thelma.

Kevin listened thoughtfully while I told him my reasoning. "But why throw the trophy away at his own business?"

"Because it looks like random bowling alley trash," I said. "If anyone asked later, he could say he'd thrown it away because Earl was dead. He couldn't leave it at Earl's house, because that would prove he'd been there. Besides, he made an anonymous tip to send police searching the wrong place. Or someone did. He hid the trophy in plain sight, which is exactly what someone wanted Sheriff Matthews to think Olive did."

"Hmmm." Kevin mulled that over for a moment. "Then all Benji would have to do is sneak out, pretend he'd never been there, and act like the trophy got damaged during the shipment. He could claim it arrived after the murder."

"He doesn't know that delivery companies keep records of that sort of thing?"

"It's possible he didn't think that far head. Most murders are done in the heat of the moment. People aren't always thinking clearly when they hide the evidence. If no one thinks to check, then voilà, nothing to tie him to the murder weapon."

"Exactly."

Nothing except the broken pieces of wood in his trash can. Which would be picked up by the county and carted away to the dump in about twelve hours along with all the other trash in Shady Grove.

"I can tell Sheriff Matthews our suspicions," Kevin said. "But I don't know how we would ever get him to listen."

"Sheriff Matthews thinks he's already caught the killer," I said. "He's not interested in investigating anyone else. I need hard evidence that shows who really killed Earl, or he's not going to believe me."

As I spoke, I knew what I needed to do. I had to get my hands on that bowling trophy, fast. "Kevin, can I borrow your car?"

"Why?"

"Um..."

After a moment's hesitation, I told the truth (mostly). Unsurprisingly, my brother adamantly refused to let me take his car to go searching for a murder weapon that I expected to find not far from the actual killer. Either the sibling love was strong with us, or he didn't want to find another live-in babysitter.

Finally, he insisted on going with me. I pointed out that we couldn't exactly leave a three-year-old at home alone.

"He's sleeping," Kevin said.

"Is that what you'll tell the judge, counselor?"

His face turned red. "I meant, we can have Mrs. Patel come over and watch the monitor."

"Right. Good call."

Our neighbor didn't answer her phone, so I tapped one foot impatiently while Kevin went over to knock on her door. What if she said no? What if she wasn't home? What if I didn't wait around to find out?

My gaze fell on his keys, resting in the dish next to the coffee maker where we left them every time we came in. It took me exactly three-tenths of a second to decide not to wait for my brother to return. If anything went wrong, Kyle still needed his father.

Kevin would be pissed, but, well, he should've known

better than to leave his keys where I could grab them. My coat still hung beside the door where I'd left it when I came in. I barely paused to shrug into it while bolting for the garage door.

Under the automatic lights sat the most gorgeous vehicle ever created. A shiny black Acura NSX—the same car driven by Iron Man in the Marvel movies. So impractical, you almost had to laugh at the car seat in the back.

The engine purred to life, and the garage door rumbled upward. Throwing the car into reverse, I slammed on the gas.

A shout rang out when I was halfway down the driveway. I pretended not to hear it. My phone rang three seconds later. Although my first instinct was to simply ignore it, the device was in the bottom of my bag. I didn't want to listen to it ring constantly until I got to the bowling alley to turn it off.

I hit the button on the steering wheel to answer via the built-in Bluetooth and didn't give him a chance to speak. "You couldn't come with me and risk orphaning Kyle."

"The fact that you think I might get killed makes me feel no better about you going on your own. Come back with my car, or I'll call the police."

"Possession is nine-tenths of the law."

"That's an urban legend. If possession equaled ownership, the state could never prosecute anyone for theft. Bring my car back."

"Sorry, brother. Not happening. I need to do this."

"Come on, Aly, think. You're not a police officer. You're not even a detective. What are you going to do?"

Unfortunately, I didn't have an answer. Telling Kevin that I intended to use my psychic powers to solve a crime wouldn't help, especially when he didn't believe in psychics. He made fun of me for three days when I wanted to visit the fortuneteller at the county fair last year. As someone neither physically imposing nor particularly skilled at questioning witnesses, he probably wouldn't believe I intended to get a confession out of Benji. I opted for a partial truth.

"I'm going to look for the murder weapon. If I find it, I'll call the police. Pinky swear."

"Here's a thought. What if you call the police now and they go to We All Fall Down instead of you?"

That made perfect sense, except I didn't think anyone on the police force had the ability to see visions when touching objects. What did I know? Heck, maybe this power was common in Shady Grove. Maybe everyone was psychic. Thelma certainly seemed able to read minds at times. Not to mention Olive.

"Aly? Are you there?"

I took a deep breath. "Look, the only suspect we have other than Benji is Wendy. And Wendy is secretly having an affair with Sheriff Matthews."

"I hope you're not suggesting that our town's primary law enforcement official would intentionally mess up an investigation to protect his girlfriend."

"No, no. I don't know. Look, I'm almost there." I turned onto the road behind We All Fall Down while Kevin finished ranting about why I should bring his car back.

Second Street housed a lot of small businesses: Kevin's office was here, but also a local accountant, the police station, Town Hall, the county clerk's office, and a life insurance agent who doubled (tripled?) as the town's taxidermist and actuary. He also notarized some documents my brother had drawn up to give me guardianship of Kyle if necessary. Clearly a man of many talents. Most businesses in Shady

Grove closed by five p.m., so other than the police station, this street was usually deserted in the evenings. Even they didn't see a lot of action. Rolling in at nearly eight o'clock pretty much ensured that no one would see me.

Since Kevin's office was so close to the small service road running behind the bowling alley, I decided to park in his shared lot and walk. Kevin's fancy car parked at his office would be way less noticeable if anyone happened to pass by than if I left it idling beside the bowling alley's trash bins.

I exited the car, shutting the door silently. Thank you, Kevin, for teaching me that if I ever slammed the door to his baby, I'd have to sleep in the backyard. The cold air made me shiver. Too bad I hadn't thought to grab my scarf when picking up my coat.

Too late to worry about that now. There was no going back.

Although the temperature had dropped so low my California-raised self used to think the thermometers must be in Celsius, the roads and pathways were thankfully clear of snow. It would be tough to be stealthy when slipping and sliding and crunching my way across the sidewalk. At least Second Street had given up the small-town charm of cobblestones in favor of paved roads and concrete sidewalks.

No one was around, but I kept to the shadows as I approached the alley. If anyone in the neighboring offices was working late and happened to peek outside, I'd rather not be noticed.

Just as I'd made it to the rear corner of We All Fall Down, headlights swept over the road. I shrank back against the building, trying desperately to dodge out of their reach. The car kept moving, so I breathed a sigh of relief.

Too soon, it turned out. After about ten feet, the car

flipped a U-Turn and came back. This time, without the bright lights shining in my eyes, I recognized the driver instantly.

"Aly? Is that you?"

I gulped.

20

My mind raced. I racked my brains, trying to think of any good reason for walking down a street full of closed businesses at eight o'clock at night in the middle of January. Since I didn't have one, I went on the offensive. "Hey, Rusty. What are you doing here?"

He gestured across the street. "My place is a couple of blocks that way. I just finished closing up the shop. What about you?"

"I was...coming to see you."

"Uh-huh. That's good, especially since you had no idea where I live until three seconds ago."

Right. Smooth, Aly.

I sighed. After making the decision to trust him earlier, it was easy to do it again. I told him everything Kevin and I had figured out, ending with, "I want to dig through Benji's trash to see if he hid the murder weapon in plain sight."

"And then see if it gives you a vision of Uncle Earl's death?"

"Yeah."

To my surprise, Rusty turned his car off and got out. "Come on. We'll search faster together."

I blinked at him. "You're going to help me?"

"Why not?"

Bile rose in my throat at the thought. I hadn't wanted to ask Rusty to let me into Earl's house because of my desire to spare him this pain, and now he was going to be with me anyway. Too late, I realized that I should've lied.

"I don't know, I thought you'd say something like 'stay out of this, little lady and leave the detecting to the real men.'"

He laughed. "Have you been watching old Westerns?"

My face grew warm. "Maybe. Kyle likes the horses."

"Listen, we probably should both go home and call the police. But I know Mayor Banister well enough to believe she put pressure on Sheriff Matthews to make a quick arrest. He's not going to admit he made a mistake without hard evidence, and he would never ever throw her under the bus. Especially after she praised him so much at the press conference. To some people, saving face is more important than the truth."

"What about his nephew?"

"Doug's a good man. A great man. But he's loyal to his uncle, and he won't go behind the sheriff's back without a very good reason."

"So it's hopeless?"

"No. We need to give him one. Let's see what we find, and then we'll call Doug."

A smile crossed my face. If nothing else, it was nice not to be alone while I did this. I started for the back of the alley.

Rusty took my hand. His fingers were so warm, I wanted to rub them all over my freezing face.

"What are you doing?"

He winked. "Giving us a cover story."

Ahhh. Without further argument, I started toward the alley. Rusty followed me to the entrance, then tugged my hand gently.

I paused. "What?"

"Slow down." He lowered his voice. "We're on a romantic stroll, remember?"

Right. A romantic stroll toward the garbage cans.

Funny thing was, this actually would be nice if not for the trash smells and the murder investigation and the looming hypothermia. The moon rode high in the sky, bathing the area in a pale light. Stars peppered the sky, making a beautiful backdrop for lovers taking a walk. Not to mention the incredibly hot guy. He was taller than Sam. Thin, but not scrawny.

It occurred to me that if I were looking for someone to date, the man walking beside me, holding my hand, might make a better choice than the guy living a hundred miles away who had barely noticed me so far. After all, Rusty didn't have to hold my hand for the two of us to walk toward the bowling alley together. Even if we saw someone, which seemed unlikely, we could say we were on the date without touching. He sure didn't make any effort to touch me on the two dates we did have.

I started to tell him that, but then remembered that Rusty was the only thing keeping my fingers warm.

The trash cans were located next to a side door about four feet from the front of the building, so we had approximately two hundred feet to hope no one saw us. The giant letters spelling out "We All Fall Down" on the front of the building cast a red glow on the parking lot at the end of the alley, which the snow reflected back. I felt like someone gazing at the world through rose-colored glasses. The area wasn't terribly bright, but everything carried a pink tinge. Bizarrely, I wondered if Thelma had picked the lights.

We'd walked about two-thirds of the way when Rusty stopped abruptly. He cocked his head toward the front but said nothing.

"What's up?" I asked.

Instead of responding, he turned and wrapped me in his arms. So warm. So strong. He smelled like brewed coffee and sugar, two of my favorite things in the world. For a moment, I wanted to forget why we were here and bury my face in his chest.

Rusty touched my chin, bringing my gaze to his. Before I could ask what he was doing, his lips pressed down on mine.

Mmmm. That was—well, odd in its timing and lack of finesse, but quite nice nonetheless. Or maybe it had just been too long since I kissed someone. I sank into his arms, opening my mouth beneath the gentle pressure of Rusty's lips.

"Why, hello there!"

A voice cut into my thoughts, and I suddenly realized that the two of us were not alone in this alley. Oh. That explained a lot, actually. Cover story. Right. Rusty wasn't kissing me because he wanted to. How unfortunate. It was really a very nice kiss. With some regret, I stepped back.

About fifty feet away stood Julie, Rusty's boss from On What Grounds?, with a guy I didn't know. Slightly above medium height, muscular, but not in a bodybuilder way. He had short, spiky dark brown hair, a neatly trimmed goatee, and wire-rimmed glasses. When he grinned to have caught me and Rusty kissing, a dimple flashed in each cheek.

"Hi," I said. "I don't think we've met. I'm Aly."

"Carlos. Nice to meet you."

"Sorry, guys," Rusty said. "We just got a little carried away."

"Aly Reynolds? Is that you?" Julie peered into the darkness. "Rusty, I didn't realize you were seeing anyone."

"It's our third date," I blurted out. Technically true, but probably not helpful.

She winked at me. "Lucky you. Seems to be going well."

All the blood rushed into my face. Oh, man. Please let Julie and Carlos not be major gossips. The last thing I needed was for the entire town to hear about me making out with the hot coffee shop guy in a dark alley.

Although that would be a better rumor than "works for a murderer," now that I thought about it.

Rusty's hand went to the small of my back, bringing me some peace. He must've been able to sense my discomfort. "Hey, guys. We're just taking the shortcut to the entrance. The night is so beautiful, I got distracted."

The shortcut? I didn't know that. Apparently there was no need for stealth if people cut through this alley all the time.

"You're here to bowl?" Carlos asked.

"Yes! I love bowling!" I put as much enthusiasm as I could muster into my response. "My brother is always talking about how much he loves this place and how... shiny...the balls are."

Rusty squeezed my hand in an unmistakable "shut up" gesture. *Happy to oblige.*

Julie squealed. "Awesome! Now we can play teams!"

"You're just relieved that I can't wipe the floor with you if it's us against them," Carlos said.

"I'd like to see you try!"

"Sounds great," Rusty said. "See you in there."

I started to protest, but Julie and Carlos disappeared inside before I could get the words out, propelled by the cold into the welcoming warm air of the lobby. Not that it mattered—what was I going to say? *Sorry, guys, we can't bowl with you because I really want to dig around in a week's worth of garbage before pickup tomorrow.*

"What do we do now?" I whispered to Rusty. Was he going to kiss me again? Did I want him to?

He leaned close, his lips nearly touching my ear. "Well, if we don't want them to tell Benji that we're out here digging in his trash, now we bowl."

21

This day was not turning out at all like I'd hoped when I got out of bed this morning. The list of things that had gone off the rails was starting to get ridiculous. Now, on top of everything else, I needed to put on rented shoes—and pray they wouldn't decide to tell me anything about a previous wearer.

For a moment, I thought about asking Benji to give me the shoes Earl had worn last, but well (a) he probably owned his own bowling shoes, (b) they wouldn't fit me, and (c) gross. I had to draw the line at dead old guy shoes. Even to solve a murder. At least unless I became really, really desperate.

The place was weirdly empty, since this was apparently the hottest spot in town. Other than Julie and Carlos, lane after lane stood empty. Through the doorway to the arcade, a television on the wall broadcast footage from the earlier press conference with the Mayor. The front of Missing Pieces featured prominently behind her. I made a sound of disgust and turned my back.

Benji stood at the counter.

"Can you turn that off, please?" I gestured toward the flickering screen.

He picked up the remote and pushed a button wordlessly. The view changed, and a weather forecast popped up instead. Twenty-seven inches of snow? Starting at nine? Yikes. We needed to make this quick.

Suddenly I understood why everyone went home after Earl's memorial ended. To Benji, I said, "Slow night?"

He grunted. "The weather report scared everyone home. I was actually about to close up when I saw the headlights in the parking lot."

"Well, thanks for being here," Rusty said.

"Do you want us to go?" I asked hopefully. This would all be much easier if the alley closed and everyone left.

Benji waved one hand. "Naw. I don't have nothing better to do tonight, and I can walk home easy enough. Enjoy yourselves."

Rusty thanked him and handed over his debit card to open a tab.

"How do we get out of this?" I whispered as Benji moved toward the register. "I can't bowl."

"Relax. Now we have a reason to be here. We'll bowl two frames, you'll get a call from 'Kevin', and pretend you need to take it outside."

"You expect my brother to help me right now?"

"No. I expect you to be able to fake finding a missed call when you check your phone."

Right. I could do that. Especially because Kevin had called at least three times since I hung up on him. This plan wouldn't require much acting ability on my part.

"Everything okay?" Benji asked from his spot beside the cash register.

"Fine! Just wondering if the shoes run true to size," I lied.

"No half-sizes. They don't fit, come back and I'll swap 'em out."

The next ten minutes crawled, but finally, we got our shoes, chose our balls from the shelves, and got the electronic scoring system set up. The computer screen looked pretty daunting, but Carlos input all our info in about thirty seconds.

"Wow. Impressive," I said.

He shrugged. "We're here a lot."

That's what happened when the bowling alley was the only thing open past sunset other than the diner. We didn't actually have an operating bar within the town limits. It was prohibited forever, but even after the laws changed around the turn of the century, things kept going wrong. According to Google (yes, I'd checked when I moved here), the first bar opened in town went out of business after the owners got a divorce. The second bar went belly up after a snowstorm took out the roof shortly after opening (thanks largely to some shoddy construction) and the third closed during the last recession—weird because that's when bars usually thrived.

After that, no one wanted to take the risk. Bars in Shady Grove seemed cursed. I'd thought the curse was a big joke until I'd realized that some people here had psychic powers. Maybe somewhere, a witch didn't want the residents of Shady Grove to over imbibe.

Once I used the bathroom and ordered nachos from the food counter, I realized that I wouldn't be able to avoid putting the rented shoes on any longer. Moment of truth. I swallowed and wiped my palms on my pants.

"You okay?" Carlos asked.

"Great! Uh, does anyone have any hand sanitizer?" I didn't know if that would help, but it couldn't hurt.

Finally, I braced myself and removed my winter boots, sliding my foot into the left bowling shoe.

It felt like a shoe. Okay. The second shoe went on. Still, I was afraid that standing up and walking might trigger something I didn't want to experience. This mission was such a mess, and it might be about to get even weirder.

Rusty insisted that I go first for our team. Realistically, this allowed me to escape outside as soon as possible, but it had the effect of setting off a flurry of butterflies inside my stomach.

I gulped.

"What's wrong?" Julie asked. "Your hands are shaking."

"Uh. It's nothing," I said. "Just...I don't know how. I've never bowled successfully."

"How is that possible?" Carlos asked. "It's the only thing to do within twenty miles."

Note to self: open a movie theater. Or a bar. Olive could help me handle any curse.

"Early on, I spent all my time helping my brother. I tend to be a homebody. I like to read, keep to myself. Especially in bad weather." Which was like half the year in upstate New York.

"Guess it's a good thing you met this guy then." Julie gestured at Rusty. "He'll definitely get you out of your shell."

Right. We were supposed to be on a date. I forced a smile. "Lucky me."

"I'm the lucky one," he said.

Finally, with no more excuses for stalling, I pushed myself off the bench and went to grab a ball. My eyes never left the shoes, not even when I bumped into the weird metal contraption with all the balls sitting on it.

Nothing happened. They were regular shoes, after all. Oh, thank goodness. I remembered how to breathe.

"Here, let me show you." Rusty picked up my ball and tested it in his hand. "Okay, first of all, this is a ball for children."

"It seemed easy to throw."

"It weighs three pounds."

"I can lift three pounds," I said reasonably.

"You're rolling it down the lane, not chucking it one-handed," Julie said. "Here, take mine."

Her shiny pink ball boasted an eight on the side, which I initially mistook for an infinity symbol. That wouldn't make much sense, though, unless she owned a magic bowling ball that adjusted its weight to each user.

That would be cool.

Taking the ball, I slid my fingers into the holes, noting how much less constrictive it felt than the lighter one. Now that I knew my first choice was designed for children, that made sense. Kyle had tiny fingers.

Rusty walked me to the space in front of where you bowl. The area probably had a name. I didn't know what it was. "Look, it's pretty simple. All you have to do is take three steps, swing the ball back, swing forward, and release."

"Right. I can do that."

"You're not breathing."

Funny how the thought of throwing a bowling ball in front of three other people terrified me in a way that digging through trash in a dark alley looking for a murder weapon while the alleged murderer stood less than twenty yards away did not.

I inhaled as long as I could and immediately felt less dizzy. Rusty took the ball gently from my hands. "Watch.

Line up your shot. Sight the ball on the middle pin. Three steps. One, two, three. Release."

As he spoke he moved toward the lane, coming down into a crouch. On the count of three, he showed me how to place the ball on the ground so it would roll into the pins. He made it look so graceful, more like dancing ballet than bowling.

"Do a practice run. Here, take the ball."

"Okay, thanks." I held the ball in front of me like a shield. This was ridiculous. All I had to do was toss the darn thing and then I could go find out if Benji killed Earl. It didn't even have to knock any of the pins down. We weren't here to win at bowling.

"You can do it!" Carlos called encouragingly from his seat beside Julie.

I shot him a wan smile. Practice run. I could do this. Mimicking Rusty's movements, I swung the arm holding the ball back. My wrist swept forward.

The world around me tilted.

I stood in a strange room. Black and white tile covered the floor under my feet. I knew that tile, having seen it in Thelma's kitchen earlier. Then I saw a wooden table, a large bald head. The man wasn't facing me, but it wasn't Thelma's table. She had a floral tablecloth this place didn't. Same floors, same counters, same appliances. Different house. Meaning they were probably located in the same neighborhood.

On the table sat the same items as in the police photos. A cauldron. Chicken feathers. Candles and powdered rose thorn. This had to be Earl's house, his table.

The ball entered my vision, blocking my view of whoever sat at the table. As if moving of their own volition, my feet traveled across the floor. The ball moved upward, out of the edges of my vision. Too late, I realized what was about to happen. I tried to scream out a warning, but the words stuck in my throat. The ball raised over my head, only inches behind the man who I now realized must be Earl.

My arms fell.

With a scream, I dropped the ball. The murder weapon. Julie's ball.

It narrowly avoided crushing my foot and rolled away. I barely noticed. Another flash hit me. Not a vision, a memory. The day I met Maria, Julie was in her studio, taking private self-defense lessons. I didn't hear the entire conversation, but she had definitely been afraid of someone. A person who no longer posed a threat to her. Julie was at the police station earlier, around the same time they got a tip about where to find the cast iron skillet. Doug never said how the tip was given, or even that he didn't know where it came from—only that it was anonymous.

Julie was a baker. Strong arms. It would've been easy for her to hide the cast iron skillet with the other baking stuff inside On What Grounds?'s kitchen until she had time to break into Missing Pieces to hide it. She was also the person who made me suspect Thelma.

The only reason I didn't keep looking into her was that she'd been working. Alone with one other employee. Rusty lied.

Everything clicked into place. I couldn't believe I hadn't seen it earlier.

Julie killed Earl.

Which meant Rusty had to be in on it.

22

My mind raced. Julie killed Earl. Rusty covered for her. He'd told me Julie was working at the time of Earl's death, and that couldn't possibly be true. I didn't know why he'd protect the woman who killed his favorite uncle, but maybe he lied about their relationship, too. All I knew was that Carlos and I were bowling with killers.

I couldn't breathe. I needed to calm down. Elements starting with the letter A: Aluminum. Argon. Oregano. No, wait. Not that. What was happening to me?

"Aly? Aly, is everything okay?"

Rusty's voice penetrated the hysterical fog slowly enveloping me as I stepped back, away from the bowling ball. My feet skidded out from under me on the slick surface, and I went down on my butt. Ow.

Maybe I was wrong. Maybe he didn't know why he was covering for Julie. Maybe he hadn't put the times together. Or maybe police were wrong about the time of death. I didn't know. But I had to get out of here.

Rusty said my name again, and I realized everyone was staring at me. I wanted to warn Carlos, but Rusty and Julie were watching me, less than five feet away. There was no way for me to communicate what I'd seen in front of them. I needed to get out of here and call the police as soon as possible.

But first, I needed Rusty to think everything was okay. "S-sorry. I, um, had a stomach cramp. I should go to the restroom."

He shot me a quizzical look. "Sure. Did you want to check your phone to see if Kevin called? Make sure Kyle is okay?"

Right. The plan. The plan wherein I would leave Carlos in here with a murderer and her accomplice, my supposed friend who I had been kissing less than fifteen minutes ago, while I went out into the freezing cold to dig through the trash looking for the very item currently rolling at a snail's pace toward the gutter. The only way to get it back at the moment was to race out into the lane and dive onto the ball before it got to the end.

"Good idea!" I said, a little too loudly.

He reached down one hand and helped me up. As I brushed off the back of my pants, Julie asked, "That looked like it hurt. Want a do-over?"

Nope. Not even a little bit. I wanted out of this building, ASAP. Instead I shook my head, "Thanks, but I'll take the zero. You're up."

"You still have another ball," Carlos said. "You can make up the points if you get a strike."

"A strike?"

"That's when you knock down all the balls at once," Rusty said.

Right. Getting a strike was less likely than a jack-in-the-box popping up at the end of the lane, and I said so. Carlos snorted. "Come on. You can't give up after one ball."

It occurred to me that I didn't know how long Carlos and Julie had been seeing each other or how well they knew each other. He probably had no idea he'd come here with a killer, so I needed to play it cool until I came up with a way of getting him away from her and Rusty. Taking a deep breath, I went to the shelves of bowling balls that separated the bowling area from the lobby. There was no way in hell I was going to touch Julie's ball ever again, so I grabbed the first one I saw without thinking. Seven pounds. I hefted it, pretending to test the weight.

"You don't want to use the pink one again?" Rusty asked.

"No!" I answered too quickly. The look he gave me clearly said I needed to calm down. "That one's too heavy. This is fine."

It took all of my limited acting abilities to return to the lane, sight the pins, toss the ball, and pretend I cared where it wound up. Three pins clattered to the ground, which was honestly better than I expected. Julie cheered for me, and I resisted the urge to scream at her. How could she be so happy and bubbly only days after smashing a man's skull? It didn't matter if she'd been afraid of him, that didn't make what she did okay.

Instead, I grabbed my phone as Rusty walked over to the machine that held all the balls and picked one. He clearly had done this before. As expected, I did have missed calls from Kevin. But instead of "going outside to call him back," I faked a loud gasp.

"What's wrong?" Carlos asked.

One hand went to my mouth before I hastily lowered it. No need to overact. "It's Kyle. He's sick. I'm so sorry. I need to go."

Rusty tilted his head at me. "Are you sure you don't want to go outside and call Kevin? Ask if he needs you to come home? I'd hate to cut our date short if we don't have to. We're having such a great time."

"Positive. I have to go. You stay here. I'd hate to ruin your evening, too."

If life were a cartoon, there would have been streaks in the air behind me as I raced for the door. Once I got outside, I could call the alley's main line and ask to speak to Carlos. It wasn't much of a plan, but it was all I had. I changed back into my regular shoes in record time. I barely managed to stop and throw the rented pair onto the return counter as I hightailed it out of there.

It wasn't until reaching the front steps that I realized I hadn't taken a breath in about ninety seconds.

"Aly, stop!"

Rusty's voice rang out behind me. My heart pounded in my throat. I couldn't stop. Couldn't talk to him. Couldn't let him corner me in a dark alley. If only I could make it to Kevin's car, I'd be fine.

I ran. Made it about ten paces before a hand on my arm dragged me to a halt. That's what I got for giving up exercising after moving to Shady Grove. If I lived through tonight, I was getting a gym membership.

"Whoa, whoa. Slow down there, Speed Racer. What happened to the plan?" Before I could say anything, Rusty paused and looked me up and down. "You're trembling. Aly, what happened in there?"

"Nothing. I'm fine. Sorry to take off like that."

His expression changed. "You had a vision."

My hands went up to shield my face. "Please don't hurt me! I won't tell anyone."

"What are you talking about? Seriously, what's wrong? Come here." He wrapped his arms around me.

I struggled, and his arms grew tighter. After a moment, I

realized that he was soothing me, not smothering me. He whispered assurances and stroked my hair. The longer we stood there, the more I wanted to believe that he wasn't involved. That I could trust him.

After all, Rusty was the one who wanted to help me develop my abilities to find the killer. Why would he do that if he knew who it was, and he was protecting her? I had to be missing something.

I took a deep breath. "I'm okay. Back up, and I'll explain."

"Okay." He sounded hurt, but he dropped his arms and stepped back toward the parking lot. When he was about ten feet away, he spread his arms wide and held them out, palms up.

"You said Julie was working in the coffee shop when Earl was killed. You lied."

His face turned bright red. "I couldn't tell anyone where she was."

"But you knew we were trying to find a killer! And covering for her makes you look very suspicious."

"What?" When I didn't answer, he let out a sigh. "Julie had a stalker. She said she was going to Maria's on Wednesday afternoon. She didn't want anyone to know, so I covered for her. But I swear, that's where she was. Or at least that's what she said."

My instincts told me to believe him. "Did you ever ask Maria?"

He shook his head. "Why?"

"Julie killed Earl," I blurted out. Not exactly the way I'd hoped to tell him, but now I was committed.

"No, she didn't." He burst out laughing. "That's the most ridiculous thing I've ever heard."

His reaction was like a knife in my heart. Good that he

wasn't going to try to kill me (probably). Bad that he didn't believe me at all.

My first instinct was to turn and walk away, but with Olive in jail, I needed someone on my side. "I know. I thought the same thing when I first wondered if she'd done it. But I saw it."

The smile slid off Rusty's face. "The vision."

"Yeah. Sorry."

"I don't believe it." He moaned. "I've known Julie since she moved to Shady Grove. We were roommates until she got the coffee shop off the ground. She's not just my boss, she's my best friend. This is like losing Uncle Earl all over again."

Poor guy. My heart went out to him. I helped him back toward the steps leading to the entrance, and we sat. It was cold, but he wasn't in any condition to come with me to the police station, and he shouldn't be driving. At the same time, I couldn't leave him alone.

"Is there someone I can call to come get you?"

He hesitated. "Call Doug."

"Don't worry about that. I'll call the police after I get you home."

"Two birds. Doug will take me home," he said. "And you need to go take care of your nephew. Poor kid."

Maybe my acting abilities were better than I'd thought. "I lied before. Kyle's not sick. He probably hasn't woken up since I left."

"Right. Sorry. I mean, that's good. I mean..." He let out a sigh. "I just can't believe it. Why would Julie kill anyone? Least of all Earl? What possible motive could she have?"

"I've been wondering if Earl was her stalker."

"For the past three minutes since I mentioned it?"

"No, I overheard her talking to Maria yesterday. She

didn't say who," I admitted. "But she was afraid of someone. Now I'm sure it was Earl. Benji told me he saw them talking during League Nights more than once, and she looked trapped."

Rusty sucked in his bottom lip as he thought about what I'd said. Then he pushed off the step and walked toward the alley.

A glance through the glass front doors showed that Julie, Carlos, and Benji had all vanished. That couldn't be good. "You've got to get Carlos out of there! If Julie figures out I'm onto her, he'll be in trouble."

"Carlos was captain of the wrestling team for all four years of high school. He can hold his own against Julie Capaldi." He paced back toward me. "There's got to be a mistake. Tell me what you saw. You got a vision when you touched Julie?"

"No, not her." Now Benji was watching us through the glass, which made me realize how weird we must look standing here. I pulled out my phone and started tapping away so he'd think I was texting Kevin. "The ball."

"What?"

I grabbed Rusty's hand and pulled him around the corner, by the service entrance into the bowling alley. "When I picked up the pink bowling ball, I had a very clear and accurate vision of someone holding it up and hitting Earl over the head with it. I saw your uncle. I'm sorry. It was him."

"You're serious."

"Unfortunately, yes."

"And you're sure it was that specific ball?"

"I am. No other ball could have triggered a vision."

"I guess you're right."

"Even if I weren't, I saw everything. Hot pink, big eight

on the side. The same ball Julie handed to me. That's why I dropped it."

"In your vision, did you see the person holding the ball?"

I shook my head. "It doesn't work like that. I've got the same point of view as the person using whatever the object is. But Julie said it was her ball."

"She did?"

"Yeah, when she handed it to me. 'Here, use mine.'"

Rusty was quiet so long, I wondered if he'd learned to sleep standing up. I was about to snap my fingers in front of his face when he put his hands on my shoulders and turned me toward the alley.

"Okay. Right. I need you to go back to the car right away, lock yourself in, and wait for me there. I'm going back inside."

"What? Why?"

"That's not Julie's ball."

What was going on? If it wasn't Julie's ball—Benji? Did it belong to the bowling alley? If so, how did it get to Earl's house? The pieces didn't add up. Until my mind's eye showed me something else the exact same shade of pink as that bowling ball: a lovely two-story house and pretty much everything inside.

"Thelma?"

He nodded.

"That doesn't make sense," I said. "She was getting plastic surgery when Earl died."

"She was—What?"

"Yeah. Don't tell anyone. But if not Julie and not Thelma, who?"

"The only other person who has access to everyone's bowling balls," Rusty said grimly.

The missing pieces fell into place. I'd been right all

along. Benji killed Earl because he was in love with Thelma. He even used her bowling ball. But he didn't want her to get blamed, so he pinned the whole thing on poor Olive.

"Benji. You get Julie and Carlos, I'll call the police. We have to get them out of here."

"Oh, I don't think so." A harsh voice rang out from the doorway behind us. "I don't think you'll be going anywhere."

23

A shiver went down my spine at the coldness in that tone. Instead of the pleasant customer-oriented person who'd rung us up and made me nachos, this voice was filled with steel. Hardly daring to breathe, I turned.

Benji stood in the open doorway. In his right hand, he held a gun. My eyes zeroed in on it, and the world collapsed around me. Never in my life had I seen anything as dark and menacing as the barrel of that gun. All I saw was death looking back at me. In a blink, I could cease to exist.

My arms went up automatically in the universal symbol for "Don't shoot."

Beside me, Rusty did the same. "Put the gun down. No one has to get hurt."

How did he manage to sound so in control of the situation? Here I was worried that a panic attack might get me shot.

"I wish that were true," Benji said. "But we both know it's too late. I've got your friends in here, and they're awfully lonely. You should come in, make sure nothing bad happens to them."

My first instinct was to run. But I didn't know how far I could make it before getting shot in the back.

Theoretically, he couldn't shoot both me and Rusty before he got tackled, but any plan that resulted in my friend getting shot wasn't an option. My mind raced, but I didn't see any way to avoid doing what Benji told us, at least for now.

He ushered us inside, where a "Closed" sign now hung on the front door. The pinkish hue on the snow had vanished, meaning the neon sign must be off. Julie and Carlos were nowhere to be seen. I peeked into every corner, but couldn't figure out where they'd gone. It seemed too much to hope that they'd run out the front door while Benji was talking to us in the alley.

At his direction, Rusty and I moved back behind the shoe rental counter. Not surprisingly, it smelled like feet. The possibility that foot odor might be the last thing I ever smelled made me very unexpectedly sad. Almost sadder than the fact that I was about to die.

The high wood blocked us from view of anyone who might happen to drop by. When I moved around the corner, I discovered what had happened to Julie and Carlos. They both sat on the floor, backs against the row of cubbies, bound, and gagged.

Tears prickled at the edge of my vision. This was all my fault. If only I'd had a better plan. Or if I'd been able to play it cool, everyone would be safe. Benji only started watching us because I'd been acting so weird.

"As soon as you walked out the door, Rusty figured out you must've seen something," Benji said.

With a frown, I poked Rusty. Sure, I was about to die, but he'd betrayed me. "You told them about my visions?"

"It just came out. I'm sorry."

"Rusty thought you suspected Thelma," Benji said. "You're new in town, so you wouldn't know, but everyone else is very familiar with soap star Thelma Reyes and her flamingo pink bowling ball."

It was so obvious now, if my hands weren't tied, I'd have smacked myself in the forehead. "I don't understand. Why was Thelma's ball here?"

"She forgot it after practice on Tuesday night. I was going to deliver it to her after dropping Earl's bowling trophy off, but I got sidetracked."

"Sidetracked, like you had to stop and kill Earl?"

Rusty poked me in the ribs. I ignored him. We were already in trouble. The longer Benji kept talking, the more likely someone would come save us. No idea who that might be. He pulled two pairs of handcuffs out from under the counter. Before I could wonder why he had them there, he locked Rusty's hands behind his back, dumping him unceremoniously on the floor. My friend grunted before rolling over, scooting into a sitting position.

A moment later, Benji did the same to me. Oof. Rusty cushioned my fall a bit, but his knee in my stomach knocked the wind out of me. At least he smelled better than feet. Or he would, if I could breathe. Our eyes met.

"You okay?" he asked

I wheezed. Rusty shifted his legs to tilt me onto the floor. A little better. I still couldn't see what was happening, but I could hear Benji pacing around on the other side of the counter. I didn't know what he had planned, but our future looked grimmer by the second.

My mind raced. Julie knew self-defense. Rusty had said that Carlos was on the wrestling team in high school. If I could untie one or both of them without Benji noticing, they might be able to take him down. I had to get him talking again, buy some time.

"What happened?" I asked. "How did you get from delivering a trophy to hitting Earl with a bowling ball?"

"No one answered the front door, but I knew it wouldn't be locked, so I went in. I was going to drop the trophy on the back table, then cut across the lawn to Thelma's and give her the ball. Earl was there, in the kitchen. He didn't hear me come in." Benji's footsteps moved away from the counter. I took the opportunity to scootch closer to Julie and Carlos. "He had love spell stuff spread all over the table. That's when I knew: Thelma didn't really love him. He'd put the whammy on her to get her, and he must be renewing it to make her stay!"

Oh, dear. What a horrible, tragic mistake.

"I confronted him. Told him I saw what he was doing and he needed to stop. Needed to free Thelma to love someone else. The jerk laughed in my face. Told me that he'd never need to waste his time putting a love spell on Thelma. Dismissed me like I was nothing. I got so mad. All our lives, things came so easily to him. Now he had the girl I loved, and he was using magic to keep her. I realized I had to free my girl from him, one way or another."

"Did Thelma know how you felt about her?" Another inch toward Julie.

"Not yet! How could I tell her, with him always in the way? I saw the way she made eyes at Earl, knew how hard it would be to get her to look at me until they broke up. I never suspected it was all because he used black magic."

Part of me desperately wanted to tell Benji how he'd gotten things wrong, that Thelma might have been free to love him anyway if he'd just waited for Earl to break up with her. But it wouldn't help. Not now.

"Then what?" In my vision, Earl's back had been to me. "He turned back to the table, so you hit him."

"I didn't mean to kill him." Benji came into view, and his eyes narrowed when he saw me. If he realized I'd moved from where he left me, I was screwed. I couldn't breathe. I couldn't even remember the elements of the periodic table. There were...some. Definitely at least one.

"Why did you take the ball and trophy when you left?" Rusty asked, drawing Benji's gaze to him.

I shifted slightly, getting my hands behind me. Julie did the same.

"No one knew I'd been in the house. I needed to keep it that way. Do I look stupid?" Benji demanded.

"No." Scary, yes. Stupid, no. "Why did you bring the ball back here?"

"This is where Thelma left it. If it showed up in Earl's house, that would be suspicious."

"Okay. How did Julie get the ball?"

With Benji's attention squarely on Rusty, I finally got my hands on the rope tying her hands together. Hopefully Benji wasn't kinky. The last thing I needed right now was a vision. It was difficult to undo a knot without seeing it, but I'd been a Girl Scout. I'd get it eventually. As long as Rusty kept Benji talking.

He snorted. "Plain bad luck. It was on the shelf with all the other stuff the league players leave here. She just happened to pick it up when she got here, and you thought it belonged to her."

"So you walked out of Earl's house carrying a bowling trophy, a ball, and a giant frying pan?" Rusty asked.

"Nah. The pan was in my trunk from the last time we all went fishing. I found it and saw an opportunity."

An opportunity to ruin Olive's life, all because Thelma didn't love him. What a waste. He could have just told her the truth. Instead, Earl was dead, Thelma was mourning the loss of a man she thought wanted to marry her, Olive was in jail, and Benji was holding the rest of us hostage.

This couldn't be happening. I was only twenty-one years old, and I was about to die in a bowling alley surrounded by used shoes. Finally, the knot came undone. Julie leaned over and undid Carlos's ropes. She reached for me, but I motioned for their feet instead. I might be able to keep Benji talking, but in a fistfight, I was useless.

In a heartbeat, they were both free. Benji was still on the other side of the counter, where only his voice told me where he was. Julie crept to the edge, Carlos inches behind her.

"Maybe you and Thelma can still be together," I said desperately.

"Absolutely. I got a new plan. I can't let any of you go, since you know what I did. But it doesn't matter. There's going to be a tragic accident. A gas leak, here at the alley, killing every customer in the place." He spoke as if talking to news reporters, looking into the distance at an imaginary camera while clutching his hands over his heart. "Thank goodness it didn't happen during Earl's memorial. Only four lives lost. I was so fortunate to escape seconds before the explosion—good thing I was taking out the trash, huh? Thelma will be beside herself at the danger I was in. She'll comfort me and finally, we can be together. I'll use the insurance money to buy her a new bowling ball and take her on a nice, long vacation."

"That's never going to happen, Benji," Rusty said.

In a flash, Julie disappeared on the other side of the counter. Carlos followed. A yell of rage filled the air, followed by a thud.

The gun went off.

Julie screamed.

I fainted.

EPILOGUE

The next morning, the news broke that Benji had killed Earl. He'd also shot Carlos in the arm when he discovered his crimes. Carlos got four stitches, and Benji would spend many, many years in jail. At my insistence, Julie and Carlos accepted all the credit for cracking the case. After all, they saved me and Rusty. No one knew I had anything to do with it, which was exactly how it should be.

With the entire town talking about murder, Missing Pieces was busier than ever. It only took about seven random people dropping in to "just look around" before I realized that they wanted to see Olive. When I'd come to last night, police had been at the bowling alley and EMTs were loading me into an ambulance. I refused to go until Doug promised me the charges would be dropped as soon as he got back to the station.

Unfortunately, my boss had yet to put in an appearance, so I was on my own. If I'd just spent the day in jail for a murder I didn't commit, I might want to spend about three weeks showering before going back to work. My plan was to simply keep doing my job. I'd promised Sam I would open this morning, so here I was. If I didn't hear from Olive, Maria, or Sam by lunch, I'd call and see how they were doing.

Julie came in around nine. "Did someone order freshly baked scones?"

"Uh, well, no, to be honest, but those smell amazing."

She smiled as she placed a crisp white bag on the corner, next to my rapidly-cooling latte that I'd yet to get a chance to drink. A second later, a large takeout cup joined it. "Oh, I know. I placed the order to have an excuse to come over here. How are you?"

"Now that you've brought me coffee? Thinking about kissing you."

The moment the words left my mouth, I wanted to call them back. She smiled impishly. "You didn't get enough action from my baristo last night?"

"Shh!" I picked up a scone and stuffed one into my mouth, taking advantage of the need to chew to glance around the store. Unless I was imagining things, at least three of the customers had inched closer to the counter. One of them was Thelma, so no surprise there. Another looked like our actuary/taxidermist, whose name I could never remember. Probably because I enjoyed the way "actuary/taxidermist" rolled off my tongue. "We're, uh, keeping things quiet for now."

What a stupid thing to say. Now the entire town would think Rusty and I were having a sordid affair before lunch. But at least that was better than them knowing what really happened. Rusty was cute. I enjoyed his company, when we weren't nearly getting killed. If we decided to date for real, it would be nice to let things develop naturally, without the involvement of the entire town. Alas, the way he and Doug had been cozying up to each other when the ambulance was driving away strongly suggested Rusty's heart might be spoken for.

"Anyway, good for you," she said. "I thought about setting him up with someone a while back, but for some reason, I got the impression he wasn't into women. Ah, well. Carlos is sweet. And he got shot protecting me."

She was acting breezy and casual, but the longer I looked at her, the more I suspected she was putting on a good show. Dark circles shadowed her eyes, hidden under expertly applied makeup that most people probably wouldn't notice—but Julie rarely wore makeup. She wore her hair pulled back, as if she hadn't taken time to wash it that morning. Made sense. After being kidnapped and held at gunpoint by a murderer, I hadn't slept so great, either.

"How are you?" I asked. "Those moves last night—wow."

"I couldn't have done it without you," she said. "Baking is my way of saying thank you."

"There is no better way. Peach blueberry is my favorite."

"Oh yeah?" Her wide-eyed innocence didn't fool me one bit. "I had no idea."

My face grew warm. Julie was so nice. I felt terrible for thinking she'd killed Earl, even though she didn't know it. Eating her scones and listening to her talk like I was some kind of hero when she was the one who saved my butt only made me feel worse. I mumbled, "Don't mention it."

By now, Thelma had completely dropped the pretense of examining the selection of impulse buy items we kept near the register and openly listened.

"Hey, let me walk you out," I said to Julie. "I want to ask you something."

As soon as the door closed behind us, I lowered my voice. "Remember that day we ran into each other at I Will Survive?"

She nodded briefly.

"Is everything okay? I know this is going to sound bizarre, but I heard you talking about how someone had threatened you, and saying they weren't a threat anymore. For a minute, I thought Earl was stalking you, so you killed him."

She barked out a laugh that turned into a strangled sound. Tears shimmered in her eyes.

"Oh, man, Julie, I'm sorry. I don't really think you killed anyone. It's just that he bought this fertility statue from Missing Pieces a few days before we died and he was mad at Olive because it didn't work—"

"Oh, no!" She laughed. "Earl was pestering me for legal advice. Had a million questions about what happened if he hurt himself while using the snowblower at someone's house or if he accidentally took out someone's mailbox. Something new every time I saw him."

"I forgot you were a lawyer."

"Recovering," she corrected me. "Also, as I told him no less than forty times, I did corporate mergers and acquisitions, so I couldn't help. Either way, he was harmless. It didn't bother me."

"That's good." I hesitated. "Are you okay? Do you need help?"

She shook her head. "Thanks, but I'm fine. Just an ex who couldn't accept that it was over. Kevin sent him a letter for me last week, and I think it's resolved. Anyway, I've got to get back to the shop."

As she walked away, I made a mental note to check in on her in a couple of days. Not just to make sure the stalker ex stayed firmly in the past. It would be nice to have a friend in town who wasn't my brother or my boss.

Back inside the shop, Thelma stood near the counter,

chatting with our actuary/taxidermist and finishing my scones. Grrr. If I wasn't careful, Missing Pieces would turn into the hottest new water cooler in Shady Grove. No, thanks. I'd had my fill of gossip and people hanging out with no intention of buying anything. I wondered if I could pointedly offer my "customers" some tea and then remind them where to get it. Not here.

Before I'd decided exactly what to say, the door to the back room opened.

A gasp escaped me as I spun around. Only three people used the rear door other than me. Sam never came in like a whirlwind, and Maria should already be at I Will Survive. Before I'd even finished the thought, someone catapulted into me.

The familiar scent of roses and patchouli touched my nose. Long arms wrapped around me. When I opened my mouth to grunt, I inhaled a mouthful of hair.

"Olive? I can't breathe."

She pulled back, grinning from ear to ear. "Thank you, thank you, thank you. I'm giving you a raise. Double your pay."

"Agreed! A verbal contract is binding in New York," I said. We both knew I'd never hold her to it. "So it's over?"

"It's over. All charges dropped. Benji gave a full confession when confronted with Julie and Carlos's statements. And now, all of my earthly goods are yours. You saved me."

"I don't need huge bonuses or double pay," I said. "I do have a favor to ask, though."

"Anything. Need a kidney? My first-born child?"

That gave me pause for a second. An arranged marriage with Sam might be okay. Like one of those reality shows. But then I shook it off. Julie and Carlos had been right. I really needed to get out more. Just not on fake bowling double dates. Which, come to think of it, wouldn't be an issue now that the bowling alley's owner was in jail.

Olive looked at me expectantly. I flushed, hoping she couldn't guess the direction my thoughts had taken. "Can you teach me how to use my powers?"

"Of course. You see the benefits now. Ready to look for a way to help others?"

"Sort of." I took a deep breath. "I want to find out what happened to Katrina."

Did you enjoy Shady Grove? Then you'll love

The Scry's The Limit

Read on for a sneak preview

CHAPTER 1

You really had to hand it to the maker of this blindfold: no matter how I craned my neck, I couldn't see a thing. Butterflies hammered out a rhythm against the inside of my stomach. Not even my first day on the job had brought me as much anxiety as these tests my boss arranged. I took a deep breath, steadying my nerves as always by mentally reciting the elements of the periodic table.

Element twenty-three was vanadium. Element twenty-four was chromium.

"Are you ready, Aly?" My boss's voice came from directly in front of me, so close I could have reached out and touched her. Which was precisely the point: I'd come to the store to test my powers.

Missing Pieces was an antique shop that helped people find the "new to them" things they didn't know they needed. In reality, Olive Green had a psychic ability that allowed her to touch an object and get a vision of its "true owner." She made matches based on those impressions, which is why the store rarely got returns or exchanges. People adored their purchases.

The first time I entered this store, an irresistible sensation pulled me toward a gorgeous opal ring. When I put it on, I saw the death of the prior owner. Didn't just see it. I felt the car accident. Considering it had been my first vision ever —and, as a biology major, I prided myself on logical thinking—it was safe to say that wasn't my finest moment. I couldn't wrap my head around the possibility of psychics even existing, much less that I might be one. But Olive and I had come a long way, and we'd been doing experiments all morning. Hence the blindfold.

Something light touched my fingertips. Distracted by my thoughts, I wasn't prepared. The item started to roll away, and without thinking, I grabbed it. Instantly, my world shifted.

A scroll of parchment laid out in front of me. Tiny, cramped writing filled the surface, the black ink glistening. In my right hand, I held a long, feathered quill. An open ink pot sat on the large wooden table before me. Men filled the room.

Picking up the parchment in one hand, I adjusted my bifocals and squinted at the top line. "We hold these truths to be self-evident..."

With an excited squeak, I dropped the pen. The feeling of it hitting my toe through my boot told me the world had returned to normal. Alas, my blindfold had replaced the wire-rimmed glasses.

Before Olive could say a word, I asked, "You have one of the original pens used to sign the Declaration of Independence? Why didn't you tell me? Kevin would love this!" My brother was a lawyer, excited by all things legal and boring. Er, I mean...No, I meant that pretty much how it sounded.

Her voice held a trace of amusement. "Because that isn't for Kevin."

"Right. Duh."

"I take it you had a vision, then?"

"Yes! But I don't feel like it counts. I grabbed the pen so I wouldn't drop it, but then I was basically holding it the way someone would use it to write."

My gift didn't work like hers. You could hand me a hundred items, and I wouldn't have any idea who the owner was unless it came with a name tag. Instead, sometimes I saw snippets of important events in a person's life. Most often deaths, so far, but other life-altering moments, too. Like a wedding proposal once. That was nice.

"Sorry about that," Olive said. "Next time, I'll make sure you're ready."

"I'm ready. Let's keep going."

"Okay. This isn't something you'd use holding it like a pen, so go ahead and grip as tight as you want."

She set something cool on my palm. I closed my fingers around the item, trying to focus on it with my mind. The weight of the object told me it was probably metal, but the whole point of this exercise was to avoid using my five senses. I needed to learn to choose when and where to trigger a vision rather than having them come to me at inopportune moments.

Nothing was happening, so I put my hands together, allowing myself to determine what I held. Flat, smooth, cool to the touch. Some kind of jewelry. In a circle. Olive had given me a bracelet, but that's not what we wanted to find out.

To date, I'd only been able to get impressions from objects by using them in the intended manner. Sometimes that turned awkward, so Olive was trying to help me learn to channel my energy in another way. Thus far, we'd had zero luck, but we kept working on it.

"Close your eyes. Concentrate." The sound of my boss's voice soothed me as I put all of my attention into the object. "Relax, Aly. Steam is rising out of your ears."

Okay, maybe Olive's voice wasn't as soothing as I thought. "I'm trying. Really."

"I know, I know. You're making progress."

"Hold on. That's metaphorical steam, right?" Here in Shady Grove, you never could be sure.

"Yes, dear," she said. "What do you see?"

Nothing. Nada. Zip. Zilch.

Instead of admitting defeat, I slid the bracelet over my left hand. Immediately, everything shifted. The ever-present ticking clock of the store faded away.

A woman's rich, full singing voice filled my ears. An audience appeared in front of my eyes, and I looked down to find my feet resting on a wooden stage. A shimmering pink gown came into view. Cotton candy pink high heels. My matching fingernails clutched a microphone. The singing came from within me.

With a sigh, I removed the bracelet and the blindfold. "I saw someone performing. Great voice, definitely not mine."

As my eyes adjusted to the light, Olive's kind face and dark blue eyes swam into focus. As usual, she wore her long, dark hair pulled back into a low bun. Today, she regarded me the same way teachers looked at an insolent pupil. For a moment, I felt about three years old. But when she spoke, her voice was kind.

"The bracelet belonged to a performer. We're making progress."

"Not really," I grumbled. "I had to put the bracelet on before I saw anything. At this rate, I'll never find out who killed Katrina."

A little over a year ago, my older brother came home

from work to find his wife dead, the house unlocked, and no one in sight but their then two-year-old son. Police found signs of a struggle, but no suspects had ever been found.

Kevin sold their fancy McMansion outside New York City and moved Kyle north to Shady Grove, where I joined them to help out. To date, my assistance had been limited to providing child care, but when I discovered my powers, I resolved to find out what happened. Kevin deserved to know the truth.

Unfortunately, I wasn't having much luck. This was the fifth object Olive had handed me in the past hour, and while I'd triggered a vision with two of them, it was only because I used the objects, albeit one of them unintentionally.

"Relax. You've only known about your powers for what? Less than a month?" When I nodded sheepishly, Olive continued, "We'll figure this out. One thing at a time. For now, the good news is, you triggered two visions without seeing what you were using. That's progress. I promise."

"I know. Thanks." Something tickled the back of my mind. "Oh! Have you had any luck finding Katrina's stuff?"

Olive clucked her tongue sympathetically. "I'm sorry, dear. Nothing so far."

Before moving, Kevin gave away or donated most of his wife's personal belongings, finding it too painful to see the reminders. It was tough to get a reading when all I had was household items people had been using for over a year— including me. For the past couple of weeks, Olive had been using her contacts to try to find any items my brother pawned or donated before moving here. So far, she'd come up short.

"It's okay. We always knew it was a long shot. I'll keep searching the house."

"And I'll keep asking around." Olive gestured at the blindfold on the table between us. "Do you want to try again?"

I shook my head. "Thanks, but I've got to go. Classes start in less than an hour. I can't be late on my first day."

"That's right. You're going to learn all the things and become a brilliant psychic scientist."

I beamed at her. "All part of my master plan to save the world."

"If anyone can do it, you can."

The jingling bell over the door interrupted me, and I turned to find a hulking black overcoat, topped with a gray scarf and a matching hat. Sunglasses covered the person's eyes, leaving me nothing but a nose from which to guess the newcomer's identity.

My boss had no such dilemma.

"Sam!" She rushed toward the door with her arms stretched wide.

My heart leaped into my throat. Sam? Here?

Olive's son was in his early twenties, one of the best-looking guys I'd ever met, and completely unaware of the effect he had on me. He lived in New York City, was studying to be an accountant, and barely knew I was alive, but once I worked up the nerve to have a conversation with him about anything other than his mother, everything would change.

Olive didn't know I'd had an enormous crush on her son from the moment we'd met. Or maybe she did. Her gifts weren't entirely clear to me. Not that it mattered: Sam and I lived in different parts of the state. Our paths didn't cross much, an annoying fact that made it difficult for me to figure out how to get him to fall in love with me.

"Hey, Sam," I said as he started peeling off the outerwear. My voice came out in a squeak. So much for acting cool to keep my feelings secret. "I didn't know you were coming."

"Oh, I'm sure I mentioned it," Olive said. "Someone accidentally started a fire in his dorm, so he's doing remote classes for a week or so until it's safe to go back."

No, she didn't. You don't forget things like getting to spend time with the man you plan to marry. But it wasn't worth arguing with her.

A week! Seven days I might get to see Sam before he left town. Element seven was nitrogen. Highly explosive, just like our chemistry.

Going through the elements usually calmed me. Now, my thoughts sent my pulse racing even more.

"Hey, Aly," Sam said. "Good to see you. Are you okay?"

"Sorry." Blinking several times, I shook my head. "I'm fine. I just realized that if I don't leave now, I'm going to be late for my first day."

"Why is your first day on Thursday?" Sam asked.

"Snow," I said.

He nodded knowingly. Unexpected snow days were just part of life in New York.

"Only you would be sad about missing a day of school," Olive said.

"Aly's not the only one." Sam smiled at me, and my stomach flip-flopped. "Anyway, enjoy. I'll see you later today?"

"Tomorrow. I've got four classes today, and then Kyle duty."

As I waved goodbye, I resisted the urge to point out all the other things Sam and I had in common. It didn't matter. Until I got my powers under control, I didn't have any business worrying about my personal life.

Preorder now from your favorite retailer

ACKNOWLEDGMENTS

First and foremost, thank you to the amazing Kellye Garrett, for a million things, but most especially for your expert guidance and critique. I never could've done this without you. Thank you to Tracie Banister for giving me the push I needed to actually get out there and write it. Thank you to Erin Huss for being my inspiration and for help making the back cover sound like something people would want to read.

Thanks to Victoria Cooper for this beautiful cover. Thank you to Kara Reynolds and Marty Mayberry for reading through and marveling at my myriad typos. Thank you also for listening to me whine and everything else.

Always and forever, thank you to my amazing husband for believing in me. Thank you to my readers for your support. I had a lot of fun writing Aly's story, and I hope you enjoyed hanging out in Shady Grove as much as I did. With luck, we're going to be spending a lot of time here.

I hope you enjoyed this book. If so, please consider leaving an honest review on Bookbub or with your favorite retailer.

ABOUT THE AUTHOR

Ada Bell is an award-winning and internationally best-selling author who thought that it would be cool to use a secret identity when writing mysteries. After all, who doesn't want a secret identity? She doesn't remember where the idea for the Shady Grove mysteries started, but she freely admits that Kyle is based on a certain precious toddler in her own life. Ada loves Scooby Doo, superhero movies, STEM heroines, and cake. Mmm, cake.

Find Ada online at www.adabell.com, or get access to sneak peeks, news and more by joining her Facebook group or mailing list. You can also follow her on Facebook or Twitter.

BOOKS WRITTEN AS LAURA HEFFERNAN

The Reality Star Series

America's Next Reality Star

Sweet Reality

Reality Wedding

The Oceanic Dreams Series

Time of My Life

The Gamer Girls Series

She's Got Game

Against the Rules

Make Your Move

Push and Pole Series

Poll Dancer

The Accidental Senator

Standalone Women's Fiction

Finding Tranquility

Anna's Guide to Getting Even